LOVE'S CHILD

Lies, deceit and betrayal, all in the name of love!

LIZZIE CHANTREE

Lizzie Chantree

Cover image: megamix
Cover design: Lizzie Chantree

For my beautiful sister, Nicky. Thank you for being my best friend and for all that you do for me.

CHAPTER 1

The door flew back on its hinges. Lucas and his secretary, Poppy, jumped in fright at the unexpected interruption. Jemima stormed into the room and glared at her husband, totally ignoring the quivering woman at his side.

'What is the matter with you?' she spat at him, with real venom in her tone. 'You were supposed to be at Dr Lomax's office with me this afternoon. What the hell do I have to do to get a baby around here? Drag you there by your briefcase?'

Lucas looked at his beautiful wife and realised how ugly she had become. She was stamping her feet, hair flying behind her, with nails at the ready to scratch his eyes out, not even caring that poor Poppy was in the room. She had become so unreasonable in her demands that he impregnate her, so that she could have a designer baby, that she had completely lost her mind.

He shifted to shield Poppy from the wrath of his wife and sent her an apologetic smile, but she scurried out, her cheeks flaming crimson, into the executive toilets where he knew she would burst into noisy tears. Lucas sighed and walked over to close his office door, to afford them some semblance of privacy after the scene his wife had just made.

'Well?' demanded Jemima, throwing her ridiculously expensive handbag on to the floor by his desk and walking over to the concealed bar in the wall to pour herself a hefty drink.

'I didn't go to the meeting because I've been twice already and we are just paying them to repeat what they've already told us. There is nothing wrong with us,' he ground out, breathing hard to control his temper.

Jemima stared at her husband and he saw her cheeks flame red and her anger flare up again. 'I had to leave my lunch with friends early to go to that doctor's appointment with you, Lucas, and I felt such a fool when you didn't arrive. Dr Lomax smiled at me sympathetically as if I'd made up some ridiculous excuse on the spur of the moment about the absence of my husband, and it sounded half-baked, even to me,' she raged.

Lucas knew that he was supposed to give Jemima anything she wanted. But he also realised that, all of a sudden, she felt she was losing her edge. She constantly sniped at him but she was no longer getting the response she craved. He didn't care what made her happy any more.

Standing there, with his back turned to her, Lucas looked out of his office window at the glorious view. He wanted Jemima to know, for the first time since she had decided that he would be her husband, that she needed to be more careful about how she handled him. He also had to manage this situation with care, or her father would step in and control him for her. Fear burned in his stomach. Then Jemima seemingly decided to change tack and went over to take hold of Lucas's hand.

Lucas looked up in surprise at the intimate gesture, but

he stood stock-still and refused to give her the reassurance she was looking for. He was tired of this charade of a marriage and only wished he had seen the trap she had set for him sooner. He had been a gullible fool, but he wasn't about to let his wife, or her father, dictate his life any more.

CHAPTER 2

David leant on the counter of the little café they had installed in the centre of the warehouse, and a smile spread across his face. He picked up the local newspaper and reread the front cover. His own face stared back out from the page, alongside that of his pregnant girlfriend, Tilly, and a group of the guys and girls that formed the main team at EVE. He was so proud of what they had all achieved, and seeing Tilly's blooming belly full to bursting with his child made him want to pick up the phone just to hear her sweet voice.

There it was, splashed across the front of the newspaper; crime was at an all-time low and David and his team were being lauded as a vision of how things could be in the future. It was all he had ever dreamt of, and more. It amused him to think how most people perceived him; a tall, muscled man, with short, cropped blond hair and tattoos snaking up his arms. They probably thought he was a typical thug. He could so easily have been a menace, after the first twelve years of his life, where he had scraped and clawed his way out of the miserable existence his father had created for them.

David's dad had pretty much ignored him, until he became useful, able to get a paper round or run around after him, which usually involved delivering or collecting drugs. Then he would get a smack round the ear or a shove in the back if he didn't do things quickly enough. It taught him to move fast and to stay out of the way as much as possible. This wasn't easy on a rough estate where going outside was not a safe option.

David's mum had literally vanished, with no explanation, when he was very young and his step-mum, Tonia, had detested him. His little sister, Abbie, fared better, as she was actually Tonia's child, but David still saw the fear blaze in her eyes when she thought he wasn't looking.

Boxing had been David's salvation. He had filled out with muscle as a teenager and knew how to handle himself in most situations. His dad had stopped punching him under the ribs the day he knew David could hit back. Boxing had always kept him strong, both mentally, when his dad had died from a sudden heart attack, and physically, when it had come to building his warehouse. When his dad had passed away, Tonia had thrown him out on to the street and he had found himself sleeping on the couches of an endless round of friends and their families. Being away from Abbie was hard, but dropping out of school at fifteen and trying to find a job had been even harder. Luckily, he was a survivor. He vividly remembered the day he had wandered into an old warehouse and found a shabby boxing club inside. It had changed his life. They had let him stay to clean the place up and do odd jobs in exchange for a bed and some food. The accommodation was grubby, and beyond basic, but someone had given him a chance and he had never forgotten it.

David didn't want to be like his parents. It was what drove him to succeed. He had turned his life around and now helped others to do the exact same thing. His work on the estate with underprivileged kids was creating quite a buzz, and he was making a name for himself as the man to know if you had a problem child. He had a knack of channelling aggression into ambition. Years of night school and days working hard at the boxing club had helped him to become the man he was today.

Local, and now even national, newspapers had started to show an interest in what they were doing at the EVolvE Warehouse, or EVE, as they all called it. Many promising youngsters, who were now getting sports scholarships and sponsorships from big firms, had started out at EVE. Kids from the warehouse were going into football clubs as the ones to watch, and one or two had created extraordinary artworks or had been seen on television in acting roles. It was truly amazing. It proved that love and support could give anyone a fighting chance. The children here felt valued and that they had a family behind them and it showed in every move they made. They were incredible.

The statistics showed that crime rates had been steadily dropping for the past ten years, and there were many more positive, happy stories for the newspapers to print. Communities were looking after each other and families even appeared to be sticking together, with divorce rates falling considerably. People were getting happier.

David's local paper was suggesting that places like EVE were the reason that communities were working together, instead of tearing each other apart. It was an interesting theory that the nationals picked up on. For David, it was just a means of getting more sponsorship for his kids, but hearing Tilly's excited squeals, and seeing her beautiful smiling face when she found out a photographer was coming to the warehouse, made him feel grudgingly happy about the article too. Tilly was his world.

Dr Cole rubbed a hand across his forehead to wipe away the sweat gathered there. He frowned at his scribbled notes. He was so tired that his vision was blurring. He shook himself and stared at the computer screen in front of him, whilst throwing his handwritten ramblings into the over-flowing bin by his feet. He knew he was on to something big. He just couldn't quite grasp the reason for the genetic mutation he had found, and was literally ready to pick up his computer and throw it out of the window. Not that this would be worth wasting his energy on, as it would merely bounce back from the blacked-out, reinforced glass that surrounded his high-security manufacturing unit. He sighed in frustration.

The building was so inconspicuous from the outside that you could walk past it and hardly notice it was there. It was tagged onto the side of a prestigious medical facility, almost ignored as an unassuming storage centre near the back of the building. It was the inside that was built like a fortress. In truth, the two centres worked hand in hand, sharing information and working towards a common goal.

The lab centre had the latest genetic and lifestyle research and the medical facility worked with men and women to improve their fertility and help them attain their dream of a perfect family unit.

Dr Cole was starting to feel claustrophobic in his own office, but he needed to concentrate right now. He patted his hand along his overflowing desk, not once taking his eyes from the screen, and grasped the newspaper he had been reading that morning. He brought it up in front of his face, too tired to move, and quickly scanned the text.

Slamming the newspaper down and sending papers flying in all directions, he jumped up with renewed vigour. That was what he needed, fresh genes to test his theory on. Newborn babies! Smiling up from the paper he had been holding was a good-looking young man called David Love, with his arm protectively wrapped around a bouncy redhead. The thing that drew Dr Cole's attention was the size of her protruding belly.

The story said that these people helped down-and-outs to change their lives. *No one brought up like this could help change society*, he scoffed, laughing suddenly and scaring his lab assistant with the unheard-of sound. Surely there would be more girls having babies who wouldn't want them, in a place like this EVE centre for unruly waifs and strays? David and his cute girlfriend were just what Cole needed to help *him* turn his life around, he sniggered. They would be the making of him.

CHAPTER 4

Lucas walked into the bedroom. Jemima was sitting in front of her dressing table. The doors of her huge walk-in wardrobe were slung open and piles of clothes were strewn all over the usually pristine floor. She'd been trying on outfits. She hadn't made a decision, though, as she was currently clad in soft black lace underwear that moulded to every curve of her breasts and hips, which she clearly hoped would make his mouth go dry and obliterate whatever else was on his mind.

She flew at him and started hammering her fists into the wall of his solid chest. He grabbed her wrists easily and held her away from him, but he couldn't deny how his body still responded to her. He knew she must have already felt his reaction.

'Why don't you want to give me a baby?' she sobbed hysterically into his chest as he loosened his grip.

He pushed her from him and she stumbled and fell on to the bed, like a rumpled goddess. He backed away from her, rudely ignoring her delectable body, and opened the door to their luxurious bathroom suite. A cold shower would shut down both his anger and his libido. He'd never been able to see her half-naked and not make love to her throughout their whole marriage.

Jemima wiped furiously at her tears and watched in shock as Lucas walked away. He had never so much as playfully patted her before, let alone manhandled her. She could usually use a tantrum to get him into bed, as it was his way of calming her down, but this time even her best lingerie had failed her.

She was so confused by the feelings that were running through her body most of the time at the moment. She had spent the afternoon with her best friends. At least, they were as 'best' as you can get, when half of them were the sappy socialite wives of her husband's friends. The problem was that Jemima needed to keep them on side to maintain her social standing. Plus, two of the mad cows were pregnant and it was driving Jemima insane with jealousy. The fact that they were stupidly in love with their boring husbands didn't help matters, as Jem couldn't really bitch to them about Lucas when they just gushed about their own perfect, dreary, *old*, men.

The others in the group weren't that bad, but she still classed them as 'frenemies'. They were all so highly competitive, that it was hard actually to get to like them, especially when you wanted to be the one they admired most and you were competing against each other for the highest standing in the group. Jem really wanted to get pregnant before Sapphire did. Sapphire was the current queen bee.

The lunch had been a disaster from start to finish. Firstly, the two pregnant women, Daisy and Maya, were talking about how much their husbands adored them and how they spent so much time together. It made Jemima want to smack them in the face with her handbag. Secondly, it forced her to make up loads of things about her and Lucas just to shut them up.

Before she knew it, she had told them how he had surprised her with a weekend away and had bought her a sparkling new diamond necklace from Cartier. Her friends were suitably impressed and Jem had felt smug that they envied her, even though it was a complete fabrication. Lucas had been away all weekend and hadn't even bothered to let her know where he was. She had had to invite her usual entertainment round to satisfy her, as Lucas certainly wasn't up to the job.

The next thing Jemima knew, Sapphire was turning around with a superior smile on her lips and telling the girls how her husband had just bought her an Aston Martin for her birthday, while laughingly saying how she had sent it back as she didn't like the colour. Her husband had taken her out for a lavish meal at a top restaurant to apologise for forgetting that her favourite colour was black, not the smoky silver he had chosen.

Jem felt jealousy stab at her again. She was annoyed that she hadn't thought of the car idea first. She was sure that Sapphire was lying in any case. Her husband was so busy boning anything that he could find, as was Sapphire, it would be a miracle if he even knew that she could drive!

Jem glanced up under hooded lids as Lucas came back into the bedroom. He was broad, with dark hair and piercing eyes that would melt all but the hardest heart. Jemima had learnt from an early age that men often couldn't see further than her own lithe body, so she had decided to use it to her full advantage. Her father had made her realise that she wasn't important enough to warrant much of his time – unless she was impressing him with schoolwork, which she found incredibly hard, or with whom she brought home, which was why she had picked Lucas.

She hadn't realised at the time how boring it would be living with a man like Lucas. He was always worrying about work, reading the latest business news, talking to business contacts or, *'blah, blah, blah'*, boring her to death with how his day had been. He should only be worrying about keeping her happy as, after all, he only had his job because of her.

Lucas had been employed by Jemima's father for some years and had diligently worked his way up through the company. He was a demon at work and her father had spotted his potential at an early stage. He had held him back, though, to see what the boy was made of. It was only when Lucas married Jemima that he got the promotion he had worked his whole life for.

Lucas had first stumbled into Jemima's life at a company party. She was trying to get her father's attention and was looking for a way to cause trouble. Noticing how much time her father spent by Lucas's side that evening, she decided that he must be someone important for her father to give him the time of day. He never usually shared space with his employees unless he wanted something from them. He had minions to deal with the day-to-day running of his empire. She was astounded her father was even there that night. She had only gone herself because she was a shareholder and needed to keep her ear to the ground, to find out what Daddy had been up to lately. What better place to start, than befriending his employees? She also knew it would wind her father up when he found out about it.

With Lucas's good looks and his quiet, understated manner, he had intrigued her from the start. She had, when she thought back, stalked him from that point on and then meticulously set about seducing him. He wasn't the usual pushover, who fell for her beautiful face – and the fact that her father was known to most of the business community.

One fateful night, she had set a trap and caught Lucas unawares. They had been tentatively dating for a while, but she went all out that evening and lured him into her bed, at the same time making damn sure that her father walked in and found them. There was no going back for Lucas after that. He'd had to marry her, or lose the lifetime's worth of sweat and toil he had painstakingly built up within the business. He could walk away, but she knew that he loved the business and the authority it gave him; it would have taken him so much longer to make it on his own. Jemima's father had resources beyond Lucas's wildest dreams, and he was clever enough to know his own weaknesses. This company was one of them. It had grown in part because of his own hard work and he was proud of that. Lucas had told her often that he wouldn't leave until the time was right for him, not the other way round.

Lucas probably hadn't felt it was such a bad deal back then. Jemima had played sweet and innocent, but was wild in the bedroom. Surely that could only be a good thing? She had been a heady mix of coyness and charm. She'd figured out what worked for him, and moulded herself into that girl. He was such a sucker.

Not any more, it seemed. She flinched as he finally turned his stare towards her. Then she felt adrenaline flow through her veins at his triumphant stance, which was telling her that he was standing up to her at last. He grabbed some clothes from his wardrobe and dropped his towel to start dressing. Jemima's eyes widened in shock and she gasped. Lucas usually changed in the bathroom and hardly ever stood before her naked, as she would find a way to make him feel uncomfortable or on edge. But his body was beautiful and she had forgotten how much she actually liked making love to him. If only he wasn't so quiet. If he showed a bit more of this spirit, then perhaps she would be kinder to him.

She lay back on the bed and sent Lucas an inviting smile, her body flushed with arousal. He turned and looked her over at his leisure, then a small smile crept on to his face. He retrieved his phone from the dish on the side table. 'It's time you learnt who you are playing with,' he said. 'I've bided my time long enough and won't take any more of your nonsense.' Then he left her.

Jemima sat up on her bed in stunned silence. This never happened to her! She had grown bored of playing the corporate spouse, and often had to amuse herself with male companions, as Lucas's friends' wives were so stifling. Apart from Sapphire, they were about as much fun as a bag of prunes. But she had never, ever, had a knock back from Lucas, or anyone else. She had read somewhere that trying for a baby could cause stress in a marriage, but she hadn't in her wildest dreams believed that it would be this bad.

She wanted a baby so that perhaps, for once in her life, her father might finally be happy with something she had achieved. He always doled out attention to her stupid sisters and their brood of sickly, messy, girly offspring. A beautiful, well-behaved baby boy would make him crack a smile in her direction once in a while, rather than the look of abject disappointment which was usually there.

She wouldn't look after the baby herself, of course. She would have a lumpy, frumpy, au pair. She didn't want Lucas's eyes to roam, after all. Jemima would hate being fat, but would just have to put up with it and make damn sure she snapped back into her size six jeans straight afterwards.

CHAPTER 5

David gazed around his small office and was amazed at how much he still loved the place. He had originally approached the local council and asked if he could develop the site to create a unique centre for the community to use. He wanted to remove some of the everyday pressures from local parents and help the children realise their true potential. It was why he had studied during endless nights, whilst holding down a full time job, to be a qualified councillor. Now was his time to shine. The council had been happy to get rid of the 'eyesore' warehouse unit, as it was full of drug users and homeless people. Their only stipulation had been that he had to make room for the homeless who already used the place to sleep, which he was happy to do anyway.

David didn't have much money then, or now, as he spent it all on the warehouse. Many of the kids went on from EVE to get sponsorship from sports firms as future top athletes. It showed how training, dedication and support could benefit anyone. The investment was small for the firms, but the money made a huge impact on EVE and the lives of the kids and their families. Extra money came in from local businesses, and he had a feeling that after the article in the papers, there would be more of them calling him soon.

David worked tirelessly with the children, with help from friends from the local estates and surrounding areas. They had all cleaned, painted and used any skill they possessed to make the centre what it was today. Currently, it had four rooms with fitted bunk beds where people could sleep. It even had central heating, though understandably it was only used when it was really needed.

They had a big gym area in the front of the warehouse with a small boxing ring that they had salvaged. David and Tilly had driven around for days to collect donated equipment from gyms that were closing down, or from people who wanted to give things to charity. They went to house clearance sales, and scoured skips in the roads as they passed. The equipment wasn't up to date by any means, but it was functional and it was surprising how much reusable junk other people threw away.

The cafeteria was the one place that was subsidised. They had to invest in it to make sure it met hygiene standards, or they would be shut down. It did turn a profit, though. Half of the money they made went on wages for the kids who staffed it, and half went into restocking.

David had a team of thirty friends now, all volunteers. They ran classes in carpentry, boxing, retail management, plumbing, electrical skills, beauty, sport, hairdressing, and any other skill base he could find. He wanted these trades to survive and hoped that the kids would learn new abilities to be able to support themselves and their families.

He thought of his girlfriend, Tilly, and how much he adored her; from her bouncy red hair and the freckles on her nose, to her shiny pink toenails. She inspired him and had believed in him when he had had the crazy idea to open this place.

He and Tilly had been friends for so long; childhood sweethearts. They had met at school, but everyone had scorned them and said it wouldn't last, especially when he'd been forced to leave and hide from social services. It wasn't until he discovered the boxing club, and its owner, Frankie, had taken pity on him, that he had managed to see Tilly again. He loved her even more now than he had then. Then he had been a child, but today he was a man, responsible for the happiness of all these people. He didn't care, or worry. The thought of all of this pressure didn't frighten him one bit. They were his family now, one that he had created himself. He was a good man and he had been lucky enough to find his soul mate at a very young age. He smiled at the memory of how they had looked then. Tilly with her starched school uniform and frizzy red hair, but the best smile for miles around, and him in battered, ripped clothes and dirty blond hair with a pudding bowl haircut! Whatever had she seen in him?

He had never imagined he would be so excited about becoming a dad. He wished he could marry Tilly first, but she wanted a big white wedding, like she had seen in the magazines. They could never afford that, unless they took the money from EVE and the families that needed it. He knew she would happily marry him tomorrow with no fuss at all, but he wanted to give her that dream. He thought back to the time when he had found a scrapbook which Tilly had made. They can't have been more than sixteen or seventeen. She had obviously spent hours and hours, painstakingly gluing together photos she had cut out of her favourite magazines, to make her dream-wedding picture. She'd hidden it under her bed at her mum and dad's house, but he had found it one day when they were rolling around on the floor kissing each other. She had blushed and hurriedly shoved it back under the bed. But he had already seen what was on the front page and that image was burned into his soul. Tilly would only ever get the best from him. She loved the real him, the lost kid without parents or family to support him and for that, he would always treat her like a princess.

David looked up as his best buddy, Alfie, walked in. He smiled at the reaction his friend always got from the ladies. They swooned and salivated in his presence. His tall dark frame and tight curly black hair, wide shoulders and sparkling eyes got them every time. He only had to look at them and they started panting his name! He clapped Alfie on the back as he drew near and laughed at the wink his friend gave Lexi, the bolshy teenage girl with coffee-coloured skin and eyes that tracked your every move. She had just started to work in the café, while she studied with Ruby, a local shop owner, in the retail training scheme.

Lexi dreamed of owning her own café and was showing considerable skill in baking, if the rise in sales of cakes was anything to go by. David would be sad to see her go when she finally decided she had learnt enough from them and moved on.

Many of EVE's kids went on work placement in shops, restaurants and sports clubs. Unfortunately, they had to finance a battered old bus to get them there, as most of the nearest shops were boarded up and vacant. David dreamed that maybe one day his EVE kids would reopen them and bring community spirit and wealth back into the local economy. David had worked tirelessly to build links with the neighbouring businesses, to get their support in giving these children a chance. He needed their backing, as lots of these kids came to him with a bad attitude and no skills or qualifications whatsoever. David was testament to the fact that you could turn your life around, with a little help from your friends.

The children didn't only learn how to conquer their attitude and find practical new skills here. They learnt to feel appreciated, to participate in teamwork, and how to be part of a family, as some, like David, had not experienced that before. He was living proof that your past didn't need to define you. Whatever background you came from, it didn't matter, everyone was on an equal footing at the warehouse.

Alfie rounded on David and swooped him up into a bear hug. David roared with laughter as his feet left the floor. As he was six foot two, this was not an easy thing to achieve. David was used to Alfie's exuberance, though, and pretended to swoon as he landed, which made Lexi fall about laughing.

Lexi adored David and Alfie. David knew that she had a huge crush on Alfie, but she also knew full well that he was devoted to his girlfriend, Stacey. Lexi had told David once that Stacey didn't appreciate Alfie enough, which made him worry about the teenager's heart being broken. 'Alfie can choose any girl he wants, but Stacey seems to think she's a cut above everyone else, the way she struts in with her nose in the air, refusing to try my cakes in case they make her fat. I'd like to give her a fat lip!'

Alfie waved to Lexi and steered David back into his office. David's desk was piled high with paperwork and he wished Tilly could be there more often. She usually ran the office like a dream. She still tried to keep on top of things, but David kept insisting she take things easy now, as their baby was due in only twelve weeks' time.

Looking at the pile of papers, Alfie wished Tilly was back too. She had worked as a telephonist in a small accounts office after leaving school, proving so invaluable that they had begged her not to leave when the time had come. She had worked her way up from answering phones to doing the books for several clients and by this stage practically ran the company. They had trained her well, but she soaked up all the knowledge they could give her, and then used it skilfully at EVE.

Before she left, and to repay the company for all the trouble they'd taken over her training, Tilly had shown one of the girls from David's EVE scheme the ropes so she could take over. Molly was a godsend. She was bright and quick and had the office running even better than Tilly had done. Everyone was happy, especially the unnaturally shy teenager, Ronnie, who worked there. Suddenly, he was blooming too, under Molly's calming influence. It seemed that two teenagers had benefitted from Tilly leaving, which made her prouder still.

Tilly had always supported David in his dreams for the warehouse, and now the time was right for her to help him any way she could. He knew that she wanted to be there with him, helping the kids and seeing them shine. Even the ones she would have given up on, David never did. She didn't have the same level of patience with the unruly ones, but often said that she hoped she would be more tolerant with their own child. She was learning from David how to be more understanding and to see beyond the barriers the children had built up, from years of mistrust and poverty. It was the younger ones who always seemed to be smiling these days.

He knew that she had loved her job in the accountancy firm and the friends she had made there, but keeping the warehouse office running in the evenings or at the weekends had become a mammoth task. The look on the faces of the children they helped was worth it, though, when they realised that someone was looking out for them, and that they weren't stupid after all.

David hadn't realised the amount of paperwork that came with running a charitable concern and a business. He had just wanted to make a difference. Tilly had always helped out, but he needed her more and more.

The bonus was that she now got to see him for longer every day. 'And that gorgeous bottom of his!' she had said out loud, the last time she had been sitting in the office, making David blush furiously and Alfie whoop with laughter.

Dr Cole picked up the now crumpled newspaper in his office, and once again read the story about David and Tilly and their warehouse full of deadbeat kids. He focused on Tilly's swollen belly and his eyes narrowed as he thought about how to approach this task. He needed to make a call to his employer, and he needed to do it fast.

CHAPTER 6

A few days later, David sat staring out of the small window at the back of his office. It had a good view of the block of flats opposite, which had several broken panes of glass. The curved brick archways underneath were littered with clothes, the occasional person and layer upon layer of ugly, filthy rubbish.

However many times his crew tried to tidy up the area surrounding the warehouse, it always ended up the same. He couldn't help everyone and not everyone wanted his help. He'd been so idealistic at the start, but had learnt early on that he couldn't cure the world of all ills.

Thinking back to when he had started this project, he tried to recall a time when this hadn't been his way of life. He had finally got his warehouse about ten years ago, when he'd been only twenty-one and determined to make it work somehow. He just hadn't quite known how to go about it then. While he was reminiscing, two big SUVs with blacked-out windows and shiny chrome hubcaps pulled up outside. *Not an unusual sight for round here,* he mused, although the cars weren't often so highly polished. The dangerous players often had huge cars. David had taught the kids to stay well out of their way.

Two men wearing jeans and white T-shirts jumped out of the cars, and David laughed at himself. He had been watching too many sci-fi films. He had expected them to get out of the car in dark suits, sunglasses covering their faces, and guns just visible from their hip. *Not that the guns would be unusual,* he thought sadly.

He wondered who they could be visiting, as there weren't many other businesses around here. He hoped that it wasn't drug-related; he could do without the trouble. Things had been going so well for him, lately. The kids seemed genuinely happier and there was a lot less fighting on the estate from the younger children. It was the older ones that you had to look out for.

He got up and followed the men with his eyes to see where they were going. With a start of surprise, he realised that they were entering the EVE warehouse. Perhaps the news stories had generated interest from some big honchos. He hoped they were the right kind of people, and not ones who wanted to cause more aggravation.

As he entered the main hall he noticed that Alfie was shaking the hand of one of the men. He grinned when David appeared round the side of his office and motioned for him to come over.

'David,' said Alfie, his eyes shining brightly. 'These guys are investing in leisure space in the area and wondered if we could work together, to create jobs for the locals?'

David frowned, but then quickly plastered on a smile too, and went to shake hands with the first, less imposing man of the pair. He was taller than his companion, but not nearly as wide. Over years of boxing training, David had often mentored lads in the gym and could handle himself, but he'd be loath to take on someone the second man's size; he was enormous! He scanned the room and took in the fifty or so kids and adults who were milling around the warehouse, and he made himself relax. Not everyone was after a fight, he reasoned to himself, eyeing the man warily.

In the early days, many people had tried to stop his endeavour. From vandalism and threats, to windows being smashed in, he had weathered them all. The laughter and music around him were testament to that. He contemplated the man before him, and felt a trickle of unease crawl down his spine.

'Mr Love,' said the first man jovially. 'My name is Alex Wiltshire and I represent a national company that hopes to develop a considerable health-based leisure site, just outside of town. We have spoken to the borough council, and they suggested that we could find out a lot about the locality from you?'

David didn't move a muscle and waited a moment before responding. He stood, getting the measure of them and slightly wrong-footing them in the process. Alex Wiltshire's smile faltered a little, but before he could fathom what was wrong, David had led the way into his office, gestured for Alfie to follow suit and closed the door behind them once they were inside.

The office contained an eclectic mix of furniture: a borrowed couch along one wall and a long table with six chairs, none matching, in the middle. *Someone would probably pay a fortune for this warehouse look if they saw it in a magazine,* David thought, but it was necessity, not design choice here. He had to admit it had its own charm, though. The only real eyesore was his desk, with its piles of papers, sitting in front of the small window towards the back of the room. He pulled out chairs for the visitors and sank down into one himself, waiting to hear what they had to say.

Alfie appeared confused as to why David was acting so strangely. He was usually a friendly, cheerful kind of guy. But then, Alfie often joked that he never really knew what was going on in David's head, and EVE was proof of that. David knew that Alfie thought the place was crazy.

Alex cleared his throat and began to explain how their bosses wanted to make use of the waste ground just outside of town. 'We want to make it a destination for sports enthusiasts, as there is a small lake there. Our vision is to use neglected space and turn it into something quite special,' he said animatedly, as if this would make all the difference to David and Alfie.

'The area being underdeveloped and cheap has nothing to do with it?' retorted David, enquiringly, watching the men beneath hooded eyes.

Alex's face flamed red, but he continued. David narrowed his eyes. From the way this guy was fidgeting, he was getting the impression that this boss he'd mentioned would tear a strip off him if he came home without a deal. No doubt he personally got a cut, so he would need to get them on board. It had probably been made plain to this boss by the local council that they couldn't develop their site without David and his team and he hadn't expected any opposition from a bunch of louts in a rundown area. It looked like he'd expected a welcoming committee.

'No one wants to touch this area, as it's so rough,' ground out Alex. A line of perspiration tricked down his forehead and he quickly brushed it away, then steadied himself by placing his hands on the table. 'It *is* cheap land, but unless you get the right customers, then the site is worthless anyway. The area has been half-developed and then abandoned when previous businesses ran out of funds. Currently it's an eyesore. We read about your work here. This area is up and coming. The edges are being smoothed out and, with your help, we would like to be a part of that.'

'We understand that we need you,' continued Alex slowly, as if trying to get a hook on the guys on the opposite side of the table, 'but the project will go ahead anyway. We are planning to complete a huge leisure site, plus a sporting village,' he added, smiling when he saw his words hit home. David was listening now, instead of snarling at him.

'We want to move the area upscale, including updating some of the retail spaces that have degenerated locally,' said the second man, surprising David. Despite his impressive bulk, he was so quiet David had almost forgotten he was there. 'We were hoping you could help us with background knowledge of the district and a way in with the people here. In return, we'll agree to sponsor some of the children you have on your sporting apprenticeships. They will get full use of the gymnasium and fitness suites for their training needs.'

David and Alfie exchanged glances, and David couldn't hide the adrenaline he felt pumping through his veins, at the opportunity this would offer the kids. He saw Alex relax at last, quickly patting his brow with a handkerchief from his top pocket. He looked happy that they had taken the bait. Now he probably thought he would be reeling them in. David's gaze didn't waver from Alex's, to make it clear that he knew exactly what he was thinking. Alex's smile faltered slightly for a second, before he dragged it firmly back in place and reached out to shake David's hand.

CHAPTER 7

Alex tried to stand up, but the chairs were deceptively heavy. David had moved them as if they weighed little more than air when they came in. 'We have state-of-the-art medical facilities and a clinical manufacturing unit in the capital that creates vitamins and sports supplements for top athletes. We are not only a retail business, but part of a growing group of businesses that work together to make people healthier and happier. We have shops where they can spend their money, restaurants for them to enjoy themselves in, gyms to help keep them fit and, finally, hospitals and medical facilities to keep them fertile and healthy,' continued Alex, as if warming to this theme. 'We work with top athletes to assist them in achieving a better performance with our nutritionists and sports coaches and, in turn, they promote our retail products. The scheme works for everyone. It may be of interest to you, David?' he queried.

'What makes you think that?' asked David, resting his muscled forearms on the table and trying to fathom the two men in front of him.

'I thought that would be obvious,' stated Alex with some

pomposity. 'You've managed great things here, with these children. How do you get them to perform so well? It's a question our head of medical staff has asked. Do you give them supplements? Are they legal?' Alex gulped and looked agonised, suddenly, as if that last question had been only in his head, but it was too late and it had inadvertently slipped out.

'I don't get them to perform,' glowered David, his eyes never leaving Alex, while rubbing his leg where Alfie had kicked him under the table to make him control his temper. 'They're just talented kids. They get the emotional support of someone looking out for them and the chance to train. It brings out the best in them. They don't take drugs – and we don't make them take drugs.'

'Of course not,' spluttered Alex. 'I didn't mean that you were drugging them! I just meant, are they taking any additional dietary supplements which might help to raise their level of performance?'

David locked eyes with Alfie, who was now treading on his feet to stop him from getting up and taking a swing at Alex's smug face. He breathed deeply to slow his racing pulse and tried to work out how he felt about this offer to help the kids. The support with medical costs and prospect of jobs and sponsorship for the children was too much to turn down. They often hurt themselves in training and it would help a great deal to know he could get them seen quickly by a doctor. David flexed his arm muscles and Alex stared at them, his eyes going wide in awe.

'The raised level of performance comes from blood, sweat and tears. If you have a talent and it is nurtured, then you can work hard and improve your game,' he said in a measured tone, whilst standing up and holding out a hand to shake those of the men before him, making them follow suit and leaving them no choice but to get up to leave. Alex gingerly took David's hand as if he hoped that it wouldn't crush his fingers when he returned the handshake.

'We'll certainly think over your unexpected offer, but we would need to discuss it with the kids and mentors to see what they think of a big development nearby. But the potential for all of us certainly sounds like something to consider.'

Alex gave it one last shot with David before he left. He seemed to have finally realised that this guy was smarter than he looked, and David guessed that unless Alex wanted to lose his job, there was no way he was going back to the office without at least securing some sort of agreement from David. It made him curious as to why this particular development was so important, when he was sure they could have chosen any number of rundown areas within a fifty mile radius.

'The medical side of our business is interested in studying what you have achieved here,' Alex said, before David could walk away. David turned back to listen. 'You manage to help children channel aggression and achieve great results. It's something that many people aspire to.' He looked at David's attractive, angular face and short blond hair and mentioned how else he could be of use to them. 'With looks like yours, you could be the face of the campaign to promote the sporting village. Especially if locals already know you get results with your training schemes. It could be worth a lot of money to you.'

Alfie snorted into his arm when Alex said how *promising* David was, while David's cheeks grew uncomfortably red at the unexpected compliment. He had no time for his own appearance, but there was no getting away from the fact that he had an ok face and the toned body of an athlete. If he hadn't got so many boxing scars and if his nose wasn't a tiny bit wonky from when he'd lost that fight to Big Nate, then Tilly always said he could be coining it in as a male model. Not that he would ever be seen dead in a poncey pair of labelled boxers, smirked David. He'd be using them to wipe up the blood of the guy he had just floored instead.

David ignored the compliment, *and* Alfie's sniggering, and shook his head. 'I don't think modelling is for me, but I will discuss your ideas with the kids. Although perhaps you might like to consider Alfie here, seeing as he's always looking in the mirror,' he joked, giving Alfie a sly wink and earning himself another swift kick to the shins for his trouble. 'I'm happy for your team to come in and see what we do here. If our being involved helps other communities to turn things around, then that's great.'

That evening David curled his arm around Tilly on the sofa and pulled her closer into his embrace. Her hair smelt like fresh strawberries and he snuggled into her, kissing her forehead. 'Well?' he asked. 'What do you think of the shopping and sports centre idea?'

Tilly was admiring the way David's muscles flexed when he held her and wasn't really paying attention to what he was saying, until he gently nipped her ear and she squealed in protest, wriggling in his lap and making him draw breath sharply at the effect her writhing was having on his groin.

She turned to face him and he could see immediately that she was excited by the idea of the building plans. He wasn't surprised, as they had been saying for years how different the vicinity would be, if only someone would give it a chance and give the locals an opportunity to better themselves. 'You need more help, David,' she said slowly, whilst dropping butterfly kisses on to the side of his face. 'The investment from sponsorship alone could allow us to run the centre for years. Plus, the site was abandoned mid-build. It's enough to make anyone coming into the area turn round and run away as fast as they can. It looks like a complete mess. Any improvement must be worth a shot. The new builders could probably have it up and running pretty quickly if they put a big team on it. Think how amazing that would be for everyone.'

She stopped kissing him and picked up the mug of steaming tea on the side table, blowing on it to cool it down. Taking a tentative sip, she sighed and put her feet up on David's lap. 'There has definitely been a change lately, don't you think? I really believe your theory is right. We haven't had so many unwanted or badly treated kids. They seem to be from loving homes. The parents can't find work and the kids are bored, but they don't appear to be hurt or unhappy.'

David thought about what Tilly had said and knew she was right. They used to have many one-parent families whose children were deemed a nuisance, or two parents who couldn't stand the sight of their kids. That was why they took refuge at the EVE warehouse. Nowadays, though, kids had parents popping in to see how they were, whether they had one parent or two; they seemed to want to know where their children were and how they were getting on. Some were grateful for the work David and his team did, others were not, but most got used to it in the end. David had shared his thoughts on this with everyone at the centre, but they had agreed to keep it to themselves for now. Outsiders knowing their secret could only mean trouble and the centre was flourishing.

'Let's give the builders a chance,' said Tilly. 'I spoke to Stacey earlier and she is jumping up and down with excitement. She says that nothing interesting ever happens around here, unless it's someone getting punched in the face.' Tilly held up her hands at David's surprised expression, 'She was only joking! Stacey would just like there to be more shops, and a gym that she can actually pose in would be right up her street.'

David laughed at this and tickled Tilly's pink polished toes, making her slosh tea on to the sofa. 'Okay, you win,' he decided, 'we're in.'

Lucas sighed deeply and wondered how he had ever got himself into this mess. He used to be strong and have belief in himself, but Jemima had long ago worn him down. The only light in his life at the moment was Poppy. She'd worked for him for five years, and he knew it was such a cliché, but she was the one person in his life who backed him up on almost everything, not just work. That should have been Jemima's job, but she had given up on him, and their marriage, as soon as she found out that her father wasn't going to be popping into their house every five minutes to see how domesticated his daughter had become.

Poppy was quiet and unassuming. He had fallen in love with her without even noticing. Every moment with her was a revelation of how his life could have been. It broke his heart that he was married to Jemima, whom he no longer cared for.

Jemima wasn't interested in him, he knew. She was just a child craving the attention of her father. Lucas understood that he wouldn't be the Managing Director of MAZE Enterprises without Jem, but he was pretty sure that her father was astute enough to know Lucas was the man for the job, with or without her.

His fate had been sealed years ago, when Jemima had set him up so that her father found them in bed together. He was sure, now, that was what she had done. Her father, Edward, or Teddy as he insisted they call him, had made sure that they got married after that. Although Lucas wasn't a ruthless man, he was intelligent enough to know that marrying her was beneficial for him too. He had worked hard to prove himself indispensable to Jem's father for years. She had just made the inevitable happen faster. Teddy never did anything that didn't work for him personally, or for his beloved company, so Lucas was pretty sure that he wanted them together anyway.

Poppy was the real spanner in the works. Lucas had never been unfaithful to anyone before in his life, but still he found himself finding excuses to work late with her until he had finally managed to seduce her – in his office, of all places! He was ashamed of his actions, but Jemima had killed off any affection he had ever felt for her a long time ago. He just wished that she would find someone else and go and make their life a misery instead, leaving him alone.

Lucas was getting to the point where he wanted to leave the company. But his fate was tied up with Teddy now and it was taking time to find a suitable way out. He felt sure that if Teddy found out about Poppy, he would plan a way to get rid of her. The thought made him feel physically sick inside, and at a loss about what to do. Lucas had learnt over the years that Teddy wasn't soft and cuddly, like his name suggested: he was sharp, cruel and ruthless. Lucas had seen how he ran his empire. He was personable and even likeable when he wanted to be. But when he didn't...

Seated behind her desk, Poppy brushed her shoulder-length brown hair out of her eyes and grimaced as she recalled the way Jemima had all but dismissed her. She'd virtually demanded that Lucas impregnate her and give her the status symbol she craved, without caring which of the staff heard her. It was all so embarrassing. Poppy felt so plain and unattractive next to Jemima. It just wasn't fair.

Poppy had sometimes tried to find the strength to stand up to her, but it never seemed to materialise in time, leaving her frustrated and angry with herself for being so weak. *She would have to find the courage soon, though,* she thought to herself. She was pregnant with Lucas's child – and she hadn't found the right time to tell him yet.

Poppy wasn't a home wrecker and she hated herself for the situation she found herself in. She loved Lucas, but he was married. That would normally have made him completely out of bounds, as far as she was concerned. She knew there were lots of predatory women out there who actively sought out married men for the fun of it, but she wasn't one of them. She wasn't sure how their relationship had even gone from working together to falling in love, as it had happened so gradually. He had been unhappy for such a long time, but he should have sorted out his relationship with Jemima first, before he even touched Poppy. *She had been so weak,* she chided herself, *the moment he had touched her, she had been lost.*

Every time she thought of what she was doing with Lucas, a wave of self-loathing washed over her, but the way she felt about him was too strong to ignore. Tears sprang to her eyes and she angrily brushed them away with the back of her hand. Her family would be horrified to find out she was pregnant with a married man's baby. They would disown her, she was sure. But if she tried to end it with Lucas and run away, he would find her, and she could never keep his child from him anyway. She looked at her growing stomach and wondered how long she could keep her secret for. She was now starting to show quite a bit. She wouldn't be able to keep telling Lucas she was putting on weight for much longer before he realised that she was pregnant – and with his child. She wanted to tell him herself before this happened, but needed to find the right way.

CHAPTER 9

Dr Cole slammed his foot into the poor bashed and dented waste bin hidden beneath his desk, which was full of scrunched up paper. Then he banged his fist on the table. The tests he had been working on for months were failing to show a result, *again!* He was so sure he was on to something and, if he could only prove it, his name would go down in history. He was sure that Mother Nature was having a good laugh at his expense. He couldn't be wrong about this, could he?

His boss had arranged for him to meet David, the man he had seen in the paper that day. The guy had managed to get numerous children out of the troubled estate and turn a few of them into decent athletes, even with ancient equipment and, apparently, no substance abuse. Dr Cole certainly didn't believe that! He was interested in how this was achieved, but also in the number of babies that were coming out of the estate – especially the girl with the red hair in the photo. She looked as if she was going to be full term fairly soon.

The global birth rate had dropped dramatically in the last ten years and people were falling over themselves to get IVF. Dr Cole's employers had jumped on the bandwagon and now had three high-tech hospitals where families could be pampered and cared for, whilst being pumped full of their own brand of drugs. Only if you could afford it, mind. The problem for the parent company, MAZE, and Dr Cole, was that the normal way of using IVF didn't seem to be working. His boss had threatened to tear his head off if he didn't find a solution and he was getting increasingly desperate. Then he had noticed this mutation.

The mutation had interested his boss enough to appease him for now, but that wouldn't last forever. The government was frantically trying to scramble together money to invest in IVF, but in all honesty, it was probably delighted that, for once, the population wasn't booming and it wouldn't have to worry so much about overcrowding for the time being. There had been more concern about having to limit the numbers of children people could have in certain communities, where they just couldn't cope with the cost of living. A supposedly secret department had even been set up to research the problem. They obviously didn't know about the contacts Dr Cole's boss had everywhere. Dr Cole was determined to be the one to find out what was happening first.

He slammed a fistful of papers down on his desk in frustration. There was a trend to the current birth rate and it was in definite decline. He had been correlating the data for seven years now, and he feared time was running out for him to produce a tangible result.

Crime rates were dropping among younger children. The figures recorded for under ten-year-olds, usually quite high, especially in tough areas, were astounding. The kids seemed sunnier, happier, less argumentative and more eager to learn. He just couldn't understand it. Unless there was a new happiness drug that made them nicer to each other nowadays? Did angry children suddenly not want to harm each other, and steal from people who had things they wanted? He really could not fathom it. That, added to the fact that there were now fewer children being born each year, made serious study and testing imperative.

Supposing the birth rate continued to drop? In a few hundred years, there might be nobody left. He rubbed his tired eyes and wondered again if there could be a virus that left couples infertile. He had tried every strain of virus they were currently aware of, but it was a dead end at every turn.

Dr Cole needed to start testing new subjects, and he had to get on to it right away. He had been given an extension every year so far for seven years, because the statistics kept dropping, but he knew that it was time for him to face replacement if he didn't solve this now. The company he worked for didn't tolerate failure. It usually eradicated it before it became a problem. Dr Cole was getting desperate. His life was in danger, and he would now use any means to survive.

The company had it made crystal clear that he was to solve this puzzle, but it had been very vague as to what methods he had at his disposal. If there was a drug being used by this David Love and his delinquent kids, then he needed to be the first to find out about it. Women were still getting pregnant here and there. *It must be a drug!* he fumed. Perhaps that was causing the genetic mutation. He had to get in there to find out.

He swept the pile of newspapers off his desk. The

article featuring David's photo landed face up on the floor, almost jeering at him. Dr Cole ground his foot into the picture, and decided that this guy was definitely a good place to start.

CHAPTER 10

Lucas was worried. He frowned at the appointment list on the iPad sitting on the desk in front of him and grimaced as he took a gulp of the now lukewarm coffee Poppy had placed there earlier. Jemima, instead of listening when he had tentatively suggested one evening that maybe they would be happier apart, had suddenly begun to hang on his every word and be overtly nice to him. Part of him, the bit that was below his waistline, responded to her in a very primal way. To have a woman like Jem bow to your every need was empowering and intoxicating, but beyond that was his sweet Poppy, and how he now felt for her. Now really wasn't the time to be driven by his penis.

Lucas knew that Jemima was only being attentive to him because she wanted a baby, and had finally realised that she had pushed him too far. She had lost him. He didn't want to be anywhere near her, or try to please her any more, and obviously didn't care where she went or who she went with. For some reason, in the same way Jem craved her father's attention, she found Lucas more intriguing when he wasn't interested in her. He'd still slept with her occasionally to shut her up about this baby business, but that hadn't happened for months. He'd found it increasingly difficult to be near her, as he loved Poppy. His body still responded to Jem on a very basic level, but more and more, he found himself making excuses to avoid physical contact with her.

He'd watched Jemima through their bedroom window that morning. She had been walking their three dogs around the acres of land that surrounded the house. He could tell by the set of her shoulders that she was angry and bored again. He'd heard rumours that she'd had several affairs, but it was nothing he could prove. '*How could he expect her not to, when she was home alone on her own all day?*' he'd overheard two of her friends gossiping, as he'd paused unseen behind their table at the tennis club. Jemima had tried tennis, squash, even polo to fill her days. One of the women was giggling that Jemima had also 'tried' the tennis coach, when he came to give her private lessons, as he came highly recommended by her group of friends. His technique was to be applauded, apparently, but she still moaned about being bored stiff, they complained – before realising he was there and jumping up to give him air kisses and profuse greetings to cover their embarrassment. His pride had taken a hit, but he couldn't be sure if they were just being malicious or not. They might have known he was there all along, and wanted to cause Jem problems, or what they'd said might be true.

Lucas was always too tired or busy to make love these days, so how were they supposed to make a baby anyway? The tests they had been having at the medical centre made them avoid each other. If they'd had sex, and they didn't get pregnant, they would have to face failure all over again. It was easier to put that off and keep checking if there were any physical reasons why they hadn't started a family yet.

Lucas knew that Jemima only wanted a baby to keep up

with her friends. She had attended the medical centre for all the check-ups. She'd even had several without telling Lucas, as he'd found the paperwork in her desk when he'd been looking for evidence of her affairs. She'd cried that she didn't want him to leave her because she was infertile, but the doctors had said there was nothing wrong. Lucas had been for tests twice, but she kept saying she was *sure* there were a few more he could take. She often screamed at him that it must be his fault! She was desperate to get him back into her bed – he frowned as he tried to remember how long it had actually been. With a start, he realised that he hadn't been near her in ages.

He wondered if she had been tempted to use the polo instructor to sire a baby, but she must be smart enough to know it wouldn't work. The fallout if anyone discovered her secret would be too great a risk to take, especially with a father like hers. It would make both Lucas and her father hate her.

Her father would disown her, he was certain. Lucas wouldn't stand up for her in those circumstances either, he might even have to demand a paternity test if she ever did fall pregnant, but he'd worry about that if it happened. For now, he was avoiding her as much as he could. She said often enough that this was all Lucas's fault. She told him to see a doctor again and find out once and for all what the matter was. She'd overheard her father talking on the phone in his office to a specialist called Dr Cole. She'd tried to persuade Lucas to see him with her, by being nice to him for a while, but she'd soon got bored and begun behaving like a spoilt princess again.

CHAPTER 11

'You're what?' cried Lucas, making Poppy flinch and recoil in the seat opposite him.

'I'm pregnant,' she whispered again, her hands wringing over and over in her lap. 'I know it's awful, but I'm not getting rid of it,' she looked at him defiantly.

Lucas had never seen this frightened, but strangely mutinous, side of Poppy before, and lust ignited in his eyes. Poppy saw it immediately and responded by blushing and lowering her eyes.

'I thought you were on the pill?' he questioned, calmer suddenly but still confused by what was happening. He felt like he had been punched in the stomach.

She studied him from under her lashes and he could see that this was hard for her, before she seemed finally to pluck up enough courage to face him. 'You know when I had food poisoning? My doctor says it would have affected how the pill worked. I didn't know. I'm sorry to tell you like this, Lucas,' she waved her arm to encompass his office, wiping away the tears spilling down her cheeks with the back of her hand. 'But I couldn't hide it any more. I need to know how you feel.'

Lucas ran his fingers through his hair and tried to work out how he did feel. Scared and angry at Poppy for not telling him earlier, but mostly sad that things couldn't be different for them. He loved Poppy and hated to see her so upset. He wanted to sweep her up into his arms and let her sob and rant at the unfairness of their situation, but he knew he couldn't do that here. Anyone could see them. It was daytime and the office outside was dotted with people going about their daily work, without realising the enormity of what was happening in their Managing Director's office.

Lucas handed Poppy a tissue from the silver box on his desk and pulled up a chair beside her. It was the closest he could get without causing suspicion. Poppy had shut the office door behind her, but if he closed the long black blinds on the wall of windows that separated his office from his staff during the day, there would soon be heads bobbing up to see why that had happened.

'Don't cry,' he soothed. 'I can't promise this won't be difficult,' he said, staring into her eyes. 'But we will find a way.'

He prayed that she'd believe him. The initial fear he had felt was ebbing away and he was astounded and in awe of the fact that this beautiful little creature had created a baby with him. Something that Jemima regularly spat that he was incapable of.

Poppy really studied Lucas this time. He knew his face looked tired and drawn, with lines of worry crossing his forehead. 'I wish I could kiss your troubles away for you. I know this can't be easy for you, but I've only ever had two choices, run and never tell you, or let you share my secret joy,' she said softly.

A fierce protective streak shot through Lucas, and he felt bile rise in the back of his throat at the thought of what Teddy would do if he found out that Lucas had disgraced his daughter. Visions of his delicate Poppy accidentally falling down the stairs and losing the baby, or her life, didn't seem such a stretch of the imagination. Lucas once again cursed himself for being so weak in seducing this poor girl and bringing her into his unpredictable world.

'You will have to go away from here,' he said suddenly, getting up and pacing the office. 'If Teddy finds out about the baby, he might hurt you.'

Poppy frowned. He felt a chill go down his spine. He had clearly told her his reservations about his father-in-law, but she had insisted she couldn't believe Teddy was violent. She'd met him a few times when he had been for meetings with Lucas, but he'd always seemed very friendly and approachable. 'Surely he couldn't be that bad. Could he?' she asked.

When he didn't answer, her eyes narrowed at him. 'I'm not leaving your side,' she said defiantly, surprising him. 'We've got this far without anyone noticing. Surely it's safer for me to be near you than miles away, where you won't know what is happening? I'll have to start telling people here that I have a boyfriend who works away and that the last time I saw him I got pregnant. I won't be able to hide it soon. They don't take too much interest in me anyway. I'm sure they won't care.'

Lucas considered the options that were open to them and decided quickly that he selfishly couldn't bear to be apart from Poppy for too long. She made his days brighter and he wanted to see his child grow in her belly and be there for her if she needed anything. 'Okay. We'll do it your way,' he decided.

CHAPTER 12

Dr Cole stepped out of the SUV and took a look around at the blocks and blocks of flats that appeared to run along every dirty and disappointing street corner he could see. They all had the same grimy windows and piles of rubbish outside. He kicked an old Coke can that was lying idly on its side and flinched as the noise seemed to ricochet off the walls. *'There's hardly a sound outside, which is strange. Perhaps the area is too rough for people to venture out much,'* he said under his breath, then saw a gang of teenagers sitting silently watching him from a low wall in front of one of the blocks of flats. He quickly walked in the direction of the EVE warehouse's front door. 'I hate coming to dumps like this,' he hissed to his security detail, who were dressed in jeans and black T-shirts instead of their standard uniform of suits and ties. 'You do look sinister, though,' he chortled to himself. 'You should fit right in!'

The goon to his right inclined his head towards the door, saying quietly that it was all clear to proceed into the building, as his partner had already gone in ahead of them.

Dr Cole stepped out of the fog that seemed to enfold the place, over a pile of rubbish and into the buzzing interior of the warehouse. He had tried to dress down today for this visit in a polo shirt, but he hadn't strayed too far from his usual lab uniform of a white shirt and pressed trousers. That was as far as he would go. He really hadn't wanted to have to come here in person, but he was getting desperate and he knew he could make people trust him, he was a man of science after all. People confided their worst fears to him and if he couldn't work out how the girls in this centre were getting pregnant, then he had no hope of finding out anywhere else. He wished they had found another spot, but if visiting a place full of badly behaved kids and bribing a few to tell him their secrets was what it took, then he would have to grit his teeth and get on with it. He simply couldn't trust anyone else to get it right. The more people who knew what he was doing, the more dangerous it became.

He was a bit dazed by how bright and cheerful it was inside compared to the dark streets and piles of rubbish outside. He could instantly smell cinnamon, which confused his mind fleetingly, then he spotted what looked like a bustling café and frowned. This didn't appear to be a hovel that was dragging itself up from the floor. It was a busy community of all ages who were chatting and smiling to each other while they went about their tasks. His stomach burned with rage that his job now seemed more difficult, but he was also relieved that he wouldn't need his security detail to walk ahead of him and bar his route to any intruders. People here looked as though they could have come from the more suburban areas of this town. He couldn't see any drugs or needles lying around and everyone was bright-eyed and smiling. He frowned and quickly re-calculated his plan to work out how to connect with the owners and pregnant women here. It might not be as easy as he had imagined to make one or two disappear. He cursed Teddy Venner once again for putting him in a tricky situation and expecting him to be able to conjure a solution out of thin air.

CHAPTER 13

David glanced up from where he was teaching one of his new kids, Denny, to spar in their battered boxing ring. Denny was small for his age, and a really nice boy, but you needed to be able to protect yourself around here.

Generally, the younger kids were lovely, which hadn't been the case when David was small. Then, the little ones had looked to the big kids to become the family they didn't have. It had created gangs, which then all tried to find a way to survive by fighting. Now the majority of younger children still had parents around. Not all of them were together, but the children seemed to know they were loved. There weren't so many lost souls floating around any more for gangs to recruit.

David patted Denny on the shoulder and motioned for Alfie to take over. Alfie shot a questioning look his way, but David shrugged his shoulders and went to see what the latest interruption was about.

Ever since they had agreed to join forces with the developers, they had had to face a dozen or so different people coming in to see how things were run there. People arrived with clipboards and spoke to the children. They had notes to mark the progress of each child's achievements, but seemed especially interested in young girls who were pregnant. There were not so many of them these days. He recalled the place being full of young mums when the warehouse had opened and he had, heartbreakingly, had to find somewhere else for one or two, as they hadn't been able to cope with them all.

Ten years later and there were only a couple of teenagers who were carrying babies, plus few of the adult helpers were about to give birth, including his gorgeous Tilly, of course. It would be easy for them to bring their kids to work later on, and he was hoping it would be the same for Tilly. He simply couldn't get enough of her. Some of his mates teased him that he must be bored with her by now, though they all loved her dearly too, but he just gave them that secret smile that made them all curl up their toes in jealousy at the thought of what he had that they didn't.

It was simple, really. He didn't get bored with Tilly, because he loved her. Sure, she was crazy and temperamental at times, and she hated it when he forgot to pick up his boxer shorts from the bathroom floor, but it was the simple things like holding hands or making her truly smile that made his insides turn upside down.

'Ahem,' said Dr Cole, clearing his throat and trying to regain David's attention. His mind had wandered off to a happier place and he guessed he must have a gormless look on his face. 'I have a meeting scheduled for this morning.'

David snapped out of his reverie, but he couldn't remember an appointment being put in the planner for today. He apologised to the little man in front of him, gestured towards the door of his office and led him inside.

Tilly stood up carefully so as not to bump her growing

stomach on the desk as the door opened and David noted the sudden gleam in the eyes of their visitor. 'Dr Cole?' she gushed almost reverently, red curls bobbing up and down with her excitement, easing her stomach around the desk to come and shake his hand.

'That's right. Tilly, isn't it?' he asked, taking a step past David, who was confused at their familiarity, and the way the man was clasping her hand into a warm handshake.

'This is Dr Cole, David!' she exclaimed with almost feverish enthusiasm. 'We've spoken on the phone a few times. He's interested in birth rates and how we can help local communities with teenage pregnancies. He's trying to find a way generally to improve the health and wellbeing of low-income families. Isn't that terrific?' she asked, eyes sparkling brightly, and her hands doing that wavy thing she did when she was excited about something, almost propelling her off the ground.

Tilly was hopping from foot to foot in glee and David kept getting lost in her smile. They had a small crèche at EVE to help new mums from the warehouse get back to work, but with the new site being developed just outside town, she was bursting to share her ideas with David. 'Dr Cole told me that research shows mothers who have their children nearby whilst they are at work are more productive during the working day. They can pop back here in ten minutes and spend their lunch hour with their children. If we don't have the space here, then they may give us square footage in the retail area! Dr Cole wants to see how we have managed to get the mums here back into work, and to see if the crèche centre that Lucille runs can be duplicated in the leisure centre or sporting village.'

'Our crèche is tiny, though,' stated David. He loved seeing Tilly so enthusiastic, her skin flushed with happiness at this new project, but he didn't want her to get stressed and he certainly couldn't see how Lucille's little crèche, which only had room for fifteen babies or children, could help. Surely a big multi-national could find this data elsewhere, or hire a professional team to design the space for them?

Lucille's crèche was a recent addition to EVE, and she pretty much ran it independently from the rest of the warehouse. She looked after local kids, so that their parents could work. She used to be a midwife, but had decided to do some child-minding in her retirement and didn't ask for payment, just a few odd jobs doing around her bungalow that she found difficult to manage herself.

Lucille's two strapping sons had grown up and moved away from the estates. She didn't blame them, but her modest bungalow, one of only a handful in the area, had been starting to get run down. Being fiercely independent, Lucille didn't want to bother her sons, or ask for their help. When she had heard about David's volunteering scheme, it had seemed like an answer to all her prayers. Some of the volunteers did get a small wage, but Lucille knew that the parents around there were a proud bunch too, and didn't take kindly to charity, or asking anyone for help.

It worked like a dream for Lucille. Her little bungalow looked like a show home now. She was so proud of it. The mums and dads whose children she cared for during the day fitted shelves, painted her walls, cut her lawn and carried out any number of jobs she needed doing each week. She was the happiest she had been for a long time, and the weight it took from the shoulders of the parents whose children she looked after was immeasurable.

She had even been able to find another lady like her, and again the barter system had begun. Sarah was a lonely widow in a three-bedroom flat. Her daughter and sons had moved away too. Lucille had told David how she'd run into Sarah in a tiny café, sitting morosely staring into her coffee and stirring it endlessly around and around. Taking a deep breath, Lucille had approached the woman, seeing mistrust in her eyes at first. By the time Lucille had finished her story, Sarah's eyes were shining with soft, unshed tears and a ray of hope.

They had become like sisters over the past few months. Sarah's flat was now full of parents painting and cleaning at weekends and some evenings, and she had offered her spare rooms to two teenage girls who had been thrown out of their homes. She had announced that she was sure that with David, Tilly and Alfie's help, they would be able to turn these girls' lives around too. The girls could be quite a handful at times, but because of the faith Lucille had shown in Sarah, David was sure she would manage nicely.

He sighed and focused on Dr Cole. He might as well hear what the man had to say. Tilly still had two and a half months to get to her full term with this pregnancy and she had been really sick and uncomfortable lately. David couldn't afford private health care; it had never occurred to him to want it either. His local doctor was fantastic, but he was also over-worked, as was everyone at the surgery. Not many doctors wanted to stay around here. David didn't blame them, and most people had come to accept it. Having another doctor available for Tilly might not be such a bad thing after all. Dr Cole seemed to have made Tilly more relaxed than she had been for a while, so David would use this time to see what medicine he practiced and if his research would be of use to the centre.

CHAPTER 14

'You work for Edward Venner, then?' asked David casually. Dr Cole stopped short as if he'd been slapped and the colour drained from his face. He quickly recovered, though. Perhaps David's boxing background had given him some advantages and he could tell when a man was quaking in his boots, even if his stance was as rigid as Dr Cole's. The doctor hoped he had managed to cover his emotions very fast, and that it didn't make David more curious.

'Mr Venner?' said Dr Cole in a slightly strangled voice. David was obviously smarter than he looked. He knew David had helped all these children, but he had assumed that as he was local, he wouldn't have too many brain cells left to fry, with all the notorious drug dens about. 'Yes, he does own the parent company,' Dr Cole continued slowly. 'But I work for a much smaller branch of the business, dealing in leisure facilities and health supplements. We like to be at the forefront of pioneering research. At the moment...' he tailed off, deciding he would have to take drastic action, and leaned in as if to take David into his confidence. 'We are focusing on performance supplements.

We think there might be a common link between genetics and high achievers. We think there is a special something extra, genetically, that helps people be the best that they can be,' he lied slickly.

Why had his researchers not mentioned David's intellect? He fumed. How on earth did he know about Mr Venner? MAZE had so many subsidiaries that it would take a lot of raking to find out that they were one and the same. Dr Cole had taken a risk in letting David know he was right, but if he knew already, he must have some serious contacts to have it all worked out. He wondered if David was already associated with Mr Venner and MAZE. Perhaps that was how he had got these kids to perform. Perhaps Mr Venner was playing with him in sending him to David? He could imagine the mirth in his boss's eyes, thinking of Dr Cole's confusion. A chill went down his spine. He felt fear burn in his stomach and a wave of sickness overcame him at the thought of being one of Teddy's toys.

He mentally shook himself and tried to get a grip on his emotions. David must have just got lucky in finding this out. Maybe he had an underground contact or two, who could be useful later on. Dr Cole felt a grudging respect for David, but he would have to be more careful in his dealings with Tilly and the girls now. This hulk of a guy would be watching him carefully. He almost wished he hadn't seen his picture in the paper. Surely there were other places he could use that would be less risky? He cleared his throat nervously and continued. 'We are affiliated with Venner Trading, but we deal with human beings, not the architectural side of things. We look at how we can get the best possible performance from workforces, as well as sportsmen and women. We work out what suits them best, say at lunchtime, when they are hungry and tired, or after work, when their bodies want to shut down and relax.' He took a deep breath and thought quickly of what to say next.

'Our supplements give them a boost. We work on enhancing their natural immune system and adrenaline drives. We also help couples that are trying to conceive with guidelines on how to get the best from their bodies.' David seemed to freeze for a second at the last comment, but didn't interrupt Dr Cole, who was warming to this theme. 'Our core business covers supplements and medical facilities to help performance,' continued Dr Cole.

'Then the outer rings of the company build retail sites and sporting villages to promote the lifestyle our products offer, not only to our staff, but to the general public. A happy workforce means higher productivity. In truth...'

Dr Cole trailed off, realising from the way David was zeroing in on him with those piercing blue eyes that he may have blabbed something important. The guy unnerved him and he couldn't put his finger on why. David was watching him closely, as if his brain was whizzing, calculating and measuring every single word that Dr Cole said. 'I happened to come across an article about what you do here, and wondered if you could teach us a thing or two about how you get such amazing results,' he continued with false brightness. He couldn't afford to screw this up.

David hesitated, clearly digesting all that Dr Cole had said. He looked like he suddenly wanted to pick Dr Cole up and shove him back where he came from, but he glanced at Tilly, who was still standing close by with shining eyes, and it appeared that the man couldn't say no to her. 'I'll do you a deal,' David said finally. 'You get Tilly the best medical care for the rest of her pregnancy and I will gladly let you see exactly how we get our results here.'

Tilly raised her eyebrows at David's quick decision, but

didn't say anything else. Dr Cole practically rubbed his hands in glee. He was a biochemist and usually had little or no interest in wailing babies and moaning expectant mothers, but this time it was just what he needed to finish his research.

His latest lab was attached to the country's newest IVF clinic, and more and more of his research involved human beings. He needed expectant mums to find out what was going on. A few disappearing from round here would barely be noticed. He could hardly take them from his home ground. *And after all, it was for the good of mankind*, he sniggered to himself.

Taking a handkerchief from his pocket, he surreptitiously wiped away the grime he imagined must be building up from this place and he grimaced at the thought of having to come back. He was a man of science, not a dogsbody, but if he could discover there was a genetic trait that might be carried through successive generations, or some sort of chemical intervention that was working miracles, he would make himself rich beyond his wildest dreams and get his employer off his back at the same time. If they had what he was looking for here, it was the answer to the situation he was in. He would be lauded as the saviour of mankind and the genius who controlled who could, or couldn't, give birth.

Rising from his chair with renewed purpose, he said, 'You have a deal.'

David watched Tilly and Dr Cole wander around the centre and stop every so often to chat to random people. He noticed Alfie looking at him with inquiring eyes. Alfie whispered something to Stacey and they both walked over to join David.

'What's going on?' questioned Alfie. 'I'm not sure what these guys want from us, but it's not a bit of market research.' He pulled Stacey into his side in a protective gesture and she squealed in protest when he squeezed too hard.

'I'm not sure,' ground out David. 'For now they are useful to us. They're sponsoring lots of the kids and Tilly will be getting the best medical care, but for me,' he swung his head towards Dr Cole, who was by now talking to a couple of the pregnant girls. 'Well, there's something not quite right about that guy.'

David and Alfie were on the same wavelength that something was wrong here. The doctor had a security detail with him, for a start. David had learnt to box from an ex-sparring champion and it had literally been pounded into him what to look out for in an opponent. It had been a hard lesson, but it had never failed him yet. These guys were definitely casing the joint and were a bit too nervous to be working with the doc as researchers. They barely spoke to him but stayed close enough to be aware of his every move. Dr Cole must be important to have security, but then why was he wandering around there like he owned the place, chatting to David's girlfriend?

'What does Edward Venner want with us?' David whispered to Alfie and Stacey, drawing them towards the back of the room.

'Edward Venner!' squealed Stacey, making Alfie pull her into a fast hug and almost smother her mouth with his own. A few people glanced up from what they were doing, but they were used to Alfie's open displays of affection, and quickly went back about their work. Lexi was the only one who scowled and stabbed a poor defenceless cupcake in half, annoyed at the kiss.

Stacey flushed and shoved Alfie playfully in the chest. 'Edward Venner is huge,' she giggled more quietly, blushing at being kissed in front of David. 'He owns those posh lifestyle resorts and I'm sure he owns a bank or two as well. What's he got to do with us?'

'I'm not sure,' said David quietly, 'but we need to find out. Let's get everyone together for a meeting and find out what questions they...' he inclined his head towards Dr Cole and his goons, 'have been asking all of us. Spread the word quietly,' he said, giving Stacey a stern look. She just stuck her tongue out at him and accidently on purpose trod on his toes as she walked past.

David didn't even flinch, as Stacey was as light as a sparrow, but he smiled at his friend, enjoying the light in his eyes while he watched his girlfriend's backside sashay across the warehouse. David put a hand on Alfie's arm to regain his attention and told him to arrange for everyone to meet at 8.oopm that evening.

'I'll ask Lucille if she can set up the crèche so that people with kids can make it. If Edward Venner thinks he can use us, he's wrong,' David said. 'I let them in here because they might be useful to us and, contrary to what they believe, we are smarter than we look.'

Alfie saw a glint of steel enter David's eyes and smiled. 'I love it when you're ready for a fight. Things have quietened down here recently, and the kids seem so happy that I wondered if you were losing your edge,' he teased. 'Obviously not.' David grinned at Alfie's enthusiasm for taking on anyone who tried to upset the balance, but rolled his eyes at the fact that he'd been missing the odd fight.

Alfie rubbed his hands in glee at the thought of taking on the suits. 'This is going to be fun!'

Teddy walked straight past the reception desk and into the bright lights of the lab. Dr Cole's assistant jumped up and quickly tried to tidy the mess of papers on his desk. Teddy ignored him and strode into one of the cramped meeting rooms at the side of the main laboratory. These rooms had a claustrophobic feel about them, as if they had been thrown into the corridor as an afterthought and landed in a hunched-up mess. No one usually used them, but as Teddy walked into one Dr Cole was sitting at the end of a small oval table, looking jittery. In front of him were two neat piles of printed graphs and research.

Dr Cole inhaled deeply as Teddy sat down, as if he was trying to steady his nerves. 'What have you got for me?' was all that Teddy said, looking straight into Dr Cole's eyes. Dr Cole gulped in some air, eyes darting to the door as if he feared that his last chance to walk out of this alive was quickly slipping away from him. He looked like a man who was hanging over the side of a cliff face whilst Teddy Venner was standing there with a look of satisfaction on his face, watching him dig his nails desperately into the muddy ground.

Teddy was currently sitting and watching; saying nothing, just waiting to strike. He hadn't brought anyone with him. He didn't need to, he wasn't frightened of anyone. If he wanted a job done, then he would see it was carried out. He didn't dirty his hands, of course, but he let his people know that he meant business. They knew that if they met him alone, they were one step away from lights out and they wouldn't see it coming.

'I was right about that warehouse centre,' stammered Dr Cole, obviously unable to stand the silence any longer. 'They haven't had anyone who wants a baby that can't conceive. They aren't overrun with pregnant girls, but those who do want a baby are pregnant, as are a couple of the volunteers.'

'Carry on,' said Teddy, giving nothing away, when Dr Cole stopped for air.

'They insist they don't use supplements or drugs,' Dr Cole continued, 'but although the area is appallingly rundown, they are still producing some of the country's top child athletes. It has to be a drug!'

'But you haven't found out if it is yet, is that what you're saying?' said Teddy menacingly, his eyes boring into Dr Cole's, making him wince as if they were burning the back of his corneas.

Dr Cole hurried on, tepid sweat dripping down his back. 'There is definitely something going on there. I have managed to make friends with the main girl, Tilly. She's starting to rely on me. I think if we perhaps make her ill, then cure her, she will be indebted to me. She may decide to confide in me if I win her trust.'

'That's a lot of guesswork and supposition,' said Teddy,

resting his well-manicured hands on the table and flexing his fingers. Dr Cole was transfixed for a moment by the movement, then shook himself. Teddy hoped the man before him realised that he needed to stay focused if he wanted to get out of this mess alive.

'I think they must have some sort of 'happy pill' that makes people feel good. The families in the group are all smiles and they love their children. For such a dump, it's a contented place.'

'Basically, you think they are all on drugs and you haven't found out what is causing the genetic mutation?' roared Teddy, standing up and not caring who heard him in the lab. They were all on the same project here, and if one disappeared, then the rest would follow.

Dr Cole shrank away from the sound of Teddy's voice and used his trump card. 'Dr Lomax has been visited by your daughter,' he spoke quickly now, shaking badly. 'He runs the IVF clinic that adjoins this lab.' Teddy stopped in his tracks and was silenced in his rant.

'Your son-in-law, Lucas, has been in too,' he babbled. 'Dr Lomax has spoken to me about it, as he knows I am trying to improve the clinic's fertility rates. He's also worried he'll be out of a job soon if the birth rate continues to decline.'

'What the hell has that got to do with you?' demanded Teddy, his mind quickly working out what Jemima visiting the clinic meant for him personally. He was a man that got anything he wanted in the world, and having a daughter who couldn't conceive wasn't an option. His elder daughters were all now beyond childbearing age, so there would be no more grandchildren from them.

'If I can solve this mutation, then Jemima will be one of the first to get my help. Don't you want more grandchildren?' Dr Cole implored. 'Your other daughters all have girls. We could separate the embryos and Jemima could have your heir. A boy!'

Teddy thought for a minute, digesting this information, never once taking his eyes from Dr Cole's face. 'Is that possible?'

'Of course... It's not legal, but it's possible.' Knowing that practically everything Teddy did was beyond the bounds of legality, Dr Cole understood that this was his only shot at getting Teddy off his back. It would buy him some time. And the more people who were aware of Jemima's trips to the clinic, the more risk there was of someone outside the company finding out.

Teddy walked over to where Dr Cole sat, towering over him and casting even more shadows in the room. He looked down at the quivering man in front of him and then turned to leave. 'Do it,' was all he said as he opened the door and vacated the room without a backward glance.

CHAPTER 17

Teddy buzzed through to his secretary and told her to hold his appointments for the afternoon. He sat in the plush leather chair behind his huge granite desk and picked up his phone, dialling a well-used number, expecting it to be answered in seconds.

He was fuming that Jemima had embarrassed him in this way. She must have known that he would hear about her visits to the clinic. It was the best available, Jemima always expected to be treated like a princess. But if anyone got wind of her visits, it would be splashed all over the tabloids, plus the press might then discover Dr Cole's medical centre if they started snooping around. The girl was just plain stupid! There must have been a better way for her to see Dr Lomax. She could have called Teddy and he would have arranged a private visit. No one else needed to have known, especially someone like Dr Cole, whom Teddy really wanted to get rid of. But now he'd just have to use the man to sort this mess out.

Teddy wanted the birth rate problem to be solved by him, and him alone. He already had riches beyond his wildest dreams, but what he craved was respect from his peers. People grudgingly admitted he was good at what he did – he was an astute businessman and had a gift for finding others with a talent he could utilise – but above and beyond this, he wanted real power over those who mocked him. Everyone always seemed to know, intuitively, that he hadn't been born and bred to wealth. However much people said they admired the way he'd come up from nothing to amass a fortune, there were always some who looked down their purebred noses at him. He'd like to grind his steel-capped toe into their smarmy faces.

He knew Dr Cole was capable of working this problem out, otherwise he wouldn't have lasted this long. The stupid man thought he was making Teddy keep him on each year, but it was the tiniest progression in the research which actually kept him alive. They needed to find out definitively if the plummeting birth rate was due to an illness, a disease, or if someone was meddling with the chemical balance of the population somehow.

This problem with Jemima was just another failing on her part, as far as Teddy was concerned. She had always been a difficult child, craving affection and having tantrums when he didn't pay her what she decreed was enough attention. *She's so demanding,* he fumed.

That was the reason that Teddy had picked Lucas for her. She thought she'd been so clever, snaring Lucas and letting Teddy discover them in her bed. But Teddy had purposely spent a long time talking to Lucas that night, at the works party, knowing that Jemima wouldn't be able to stop herself from jumping on Lucas later on. Teddy hadn't expected her to plan for him to walk in on them, though, but it did show him how ruthless his daughter could be in attaining her own end. *Perhaps she was a chip off the old block after all,* he thought grudgingly.

Lucas had been selected because he was a good man. Not only that, but he was smart and extremely proficient at running the MAZE head office. He was quiet enough to keep Jemima's outbursts under control, but not enough of a pushover to tolerate all her bad behaviour.

Teddy picked up the phone, listened to the voice at the other end of the line, and then slowly explained what he needed to happen and how he wanted it done.

CHAPTER 18

David whistled loudly and Alfie called for everyone to shut up. People were still milling around and finding a place to sit on the array of chairs and beanbags dotted around EVE's main room. Then David cleared his throat and waited for everyone to stop speaking. He was pleased to see practically all of their group there, including a few parents who worked nights but had managed to swap their shifts.

Tilly gave David a comforting squeeze on the shoulder and slowly walked over to find a soft chair. She only had a few weeks to go until the baby was due, and he knew she was feeling decidedly heavy and cumbersome.

They had spent the earlier part of the evening circulating, asking everyone what Dr Cole and his team from the development had been questioning them about, but they were really no clearer about why the visitors needed EVE's involvement.

Dr Cole's occasional appearances, and his seemingly innocent attachment to Tilly, were starting to put David's teeth on edge. Tilly was so much more relaxed and definitely happier, but the more involved they became with the developers, the more David felt like it was a weight around their necks.

Work was well underway already on clearing the scrub ground and local people were making an effort to let the builders come and go without cars getting smashed or property vandalised, but it would take time for them to really trust a big company like this to have their best interests at heart.

'We need to decide if we are still happy for these guys to be coming around here,' ventured David. 'It seems from what you have all said, that they are collecting data on how we interact and get the best from the kids here, which is what they said they wanted. To find a supplement or new organic form to improve performance and lifestyle.' He parroted as if he was trying to convince himself as much as anyone else. 'They've charted what we eat, when we eat it, how we act around each other and what we say to help each other perform to the best of our abilities. It still doesn't add up. I have seen one or two of them trying to snoop into my office, but they won't find anything there.' Everyone sniggered at that. The love and support they gave each other and the results it helped them achieve couldn't be explained on a piece of paper.

'They give me the creeps,' said one girl from the back, distractedly rubbing her pregnant stomach with her hand.

'And me,' said Lexi, from her place at the side of the hall. 'They are always fawning over Tilly and the other mums-to-be. I've been watching them for days now from behind the kiosk.' Alfie gave her a wink of encouragement and earned a glower from Stacey in return, so he quickly smoothed his hand over hers in apology.

'They want to know what we know,' sighed David. 'We have kept it to ourselves for as long as we could, but they want to make money out of it. They aren't out for the good of mankind. They just want to make a profit. I knew this would happen one day, but as it was such a gradual change, I hoped it would go unnoticed for a while longer.'

'What happens if they try to match the gene, or find out what is really happening here?' asked Tilly.

David walked over to grasp her hand. 'Then we will be back to where we were ten years ago.' There was a collective murmur around the room as people grasped what he was saying, and realised how it would affect their lives. People would be having babies that weren't wanted again, if these people understood what was happening and reversed the new gene.

'I told you what I thought was happening here, because we are a small community, and I trust you all, but I could be wrong. I'm not a scientist.'

'Are you sure that it's so bad if they find out?' asked Tilly. 'Perhaps it will be good for everyone to know what is going on. Then they can see that this is not something that's bad or detrimental to any of us. It's a breath of fresh air and Mother Nature is making the change, not us,' she said, smiling around the room encompassing everyone there.

'We have kept it a secret this long, but is it fair not to share what we know with everyone else? What about couples who can't conceive? Perhaps this could help them?' said Stacey, moving nearer to Alfie. He grasped her hand and frowned at David as if he really didn't know what to do for the best, but he hoped his friend did. David rolled his eyes heavenward and hoped he had the strength to stay focused and not buckle under the pressure.

'Let's all calm down for a minute.' David soothed, using a quiet but commanding tone of voice. 'They haven't actually found anything, or we would have heard about it. They only looked here in the first place because some of our kids are doing so well in their field that people are starting to notice. What else could we do? Make them underperform so that no one looks at us here? What opportunities in life would they get then? People would take one look at where they come from and tell them to get lost!' he said. His voice was rising in volume, but he was still keeping control of his racing emotions.

'We knew that when the children started to go out into the world, they would make a difference. That is what we decided. For them to be the start of something good. It's working. They are grown from the love and support of us all. They have better skills, choices, and hopefully a better life, than we had as children.'

'We chose to have the developers here,' stated Tilly to the group. Stacey, in particular, was looking at the floor when Tilly said this, and David wasn't surprised that she didn't want to acknowledge her part in bringing them there.

'Yes,' said David, 'but we did that to nurture the bigger community. There are so many local people out of work and this is a chance for us to assist them. They don't know too much about what is going on here, but they realise that we are trying to help. That's why they steer clear and let us get on with it. We had to say yes. This thing is bigger than a small warehouse in the middle of a rough estate.'

'I don't think they care about us,' said Stacey angrily. 'They just keep out of the way because they know that you and Alfie will kick their asses if they try and mess with this place.'

〜

Everyone laughed at this and Alfie pulled Stacey into a

quick hug, making her blush and Lexi wince. Lexi eyed Stacey's skin-tight jeans and bright red top and wished with all her might that it was her that Alfie was hugging. Stacey was such a selfish cow! David had brought this community together and trusted them with his secret, but as far as Lexi was concerned, Stacey was a liability. She was the one who wanted the developers there, so that she could prance around looking stupid in her sportswear. She would probably be the one to let slip to those interfering, clipboard wielding researchers, what was actually going on.

CHAPTER 19

Teddy put his feet up on his desk and stared out of his office window. He had panoramic views of the city, but today he was looking without actually seeing anything. He glanced in annoyance at the phone on his desk, willing it to ring. The buzzing of the receiver when it finally did made him jump, and he quickly grabbed it to his ear.

Within minutes he was slamming the phone back down on the table and rising from his chair to pace his office. He was incensed! How dare Lucas treat him like this? Hadn't he given the boy everything he could dream of, including his daughter?

Teddy pictured Jemima's beautiful face, and felt a blast of fury shoot through him. No one messed with the Venner family. For the first time in as long as he could remember, Teddy felt some sort of empathy with his daughter. He would cover this up before she found out. She would be devastated. Who knew how volatile she could become if she found out what Lucas had done? *No*, reasoned Teddy. He would make sure Lucas remembered who was boss, and teach him a whole new level of respect. The stupid boy could not be seen to be running around with another woman publicly. Everyone knew, surely, that Teddy wouldn't stand for it.

Few would dare to gossip publicly about Teddy's family, but privately, he bet they would be rubbing their hands in glee. They would love to see him fall flat on his face and he wasn't about to let his son-in-law's wandering penis be the reason people scorned him. He would rectify this problem before anyone found out. It seemed that Lucas was being very secretive about it at the moment, but he wouldn't be able to hide it for much longer if Teddy's information was correct. Teddy felt his blood boiling in his veins, he was so angry. Teddy's contact had found out about Lucas's little tryst, so there was a possibility that others could too. This made Teddy vulnerable, and pushed him to resolve the matter before Lucas decided to do anything silly, like leave Teddy's daughter.

Lucas had helped to build MAZE into the multinational business it was today and Teddy respected that, but he had overstepped the line and unfortunately that meant paying a price. Teddy felt a punch of disappointment that the boy had let him down. He'd chosen him for his reliability, but it seemed that the anomaly was Jemima. Teddy should have taken into account how difficult she was to live with. It had been the same when she was growing up. She demanded attention from everyone, every minute of the day. He should have set Lucas up with a more pliable daughter and then maybe none of this mess would have occurred. But it was too late for that now and all that he could do was damage limitation.

CHAPTER 20

Jemima sat at the beautiful breakfast table in her kitchen, overlooking the sumptuous grounds of her garden, idly shredding the newspaper in front of her. She raised her toes to run them along the coat of the golden retriever who was sitting contentedly at her feet. Then she sighed in boredom.

Lucas collected his coat on the way to the front door and stopped to check in on Jemima. She knew that she looked forlorn, sitting there on her own, but he was frowning and not really focusing on her. She worried fleetingly that there might be problems at work.

She raised her head to look at him carefully as he stopped by the kitchen door. She took in the immaculately pressed trousers and casual top he was wearing. He smelt wonderful too. 'Won't you change your mind about working today?' she asked, hoping he would just sweep her up and carry her back to bed, like he used to when they were first married.

She wondered why he was wearing such casual clothes for a working weekend. He was usually so uptight that he wore a suit practically every day. 'I can't stop,' he said, quickly coming over to drop a swift kiss on to the top of her head. 'I've got a meeting in half an hour.'

'Where?' she questioned, frowning at the kiss. He hadn't come near her for ages.

'Just the golf club,' he said casually. 'They've kept a meeting room for me, as I didn't want to travel as far as the office today.'

'How long will you be gone for?' she whined, knowing she sounded like a petulant child, tears almost falling from her eyes, but not quite. She wouldn't let him see how his behaviour of late was starting to get to her. The more he ignored her, the more he fascinated her.

'Most of the day,' he said, walking back to the front door and opening it to leave.

'Can't I come with you?' she called out after him, but he had already closed the door behind him and was getting into his shiny black car.

Jemima pulled out a book from the side table and tried to focus on the text in front of her, but something wasn't quite right. She didn't usually pay that much attention to what Lucas was saying, but the clothes he was wearing, and the way he had left the house, put her on edge for some reason. She shook herself to try and get out of the fug she had been feeling lately, but nothing seemed to work.

Deciding she was fed up with this pathetic, weak side of herself she had recently discovered, she resolved to take action to get Lucas back. She jumped up with renewed vigour and ran to change into something that didn't make her look like she had been sitting indoors sulking all week.

She knew what she would do; buy new clothes, plan an exciting meal together, then she would seduce her distracted husband. He would be so pleased that she was being nice to him, he would forgive her anything. She could even play at being all coy and submissive, if that was what rocked his boat.

Sitting behind the wheel of her favourite red convertible, she revved the engine, and left a spray of gravel behind her as she put her foot on the pedal, shooting up the driveway at speed. Lucas would come home to a new, better version of his wife, and they would fall in love all over again.

Jemima smiled with satisfaction at the array of brightly coloured bags on the seat next to her in the car. She had been pampered and primped at her local salon, and her hair hung softly around her face. The new subtle golden tones would make Lucas remember what he was missing. Her toenails had been painted a deep pink blush and her body rubbed into submission by the most talented girls at the spa at the back of the salon. She felt wired with energy and ready to confront the problems she had been facing with Lucas. She was sure that this was just a blip in their marriage and that they would be back on more solid footing soon.

Checking in her rear view mirror she indicated to turn left and swung her little red convertible into the golf club parking lot. Leaving her purchases on the front seat, she almost skipped into the foyer, hardly able to contain herself at the thought of the surprise on Lucas's face when he found out that she would be waiting at home for him when he finished his meeting, with a beautiful, almost-home cooked meal. He couldn't expect miracles. She would let their chef, Sabine, go once she had prepared the basics and left them in the oven for Jemima to turn on.

The receptionist looked up and smiled when she saw

Jemima approach. 'Can I help you at all, madam?' she enquired politely.

'I was just hoping to pop in and see my husband, Lucas Trent. He has a meeting room booked out today,' said Jemima, smiling prettily at the girl behind the desk.

'I'll just take a look at our system,' said the girl with a frown. 'I schedule the calendar for all of the meeting rooms. Mr Trent is a regular visitor for golf and our executive facilities, which includes the use of meeting rooms and presentation suites, but I don't think I have seen anything for him today.' She clicked a link on the screen and the daily bookings appeared. 'I can't see a meeting for him in our executive rooms, but I've been out of reception on other duties, so he may well have been in without me seeing him and left already. Perhaps he booked into an alternative club?' she apologised. 'Would you like me to call around for you?'

Jemima felt like she had been slapped in the face and her cheeks grew hot in mortification and embarrassment. 'My mistake,' she parried, quickly turning on her heel and rushing back to her car, holding on to the door for support. Why had Lucas lied to her? She quickly got into her car and drove at speed out of the car park before anyone saw the tears streaming from her eyes.

Opening the front door and running up into her bedroom before any of the staff noticed and had a good laugh, Jemima slammed the ensuite door behind her and slumped to the floor. He had another woman, she just knew it! She hadn't thought she would care if Lucas took another woman, but it hurt like hell. She got up slowly and looked at her face in the mirror. Her perfectly applied make-up was running unchecked down her face and she looked a complete mess. The time on her watch said it was nearing six o'clock. If she didn't want Lucas to find her like this before she had worked out what to do, then she needed to pull herself together and think clearly.

She felt numb with shock. She knew that Lucas wasn't the type to sleep around. Perhaps this wouldn't hurt so much if he was. It meant that he had found someone else he wanted to be with. The thought made Jem press her nails into her palms and scream at her reflection, and she itched to pick something up and throw it through the nearest window, but managed to take control of her emotions. Her father would have another reason to think she was a failure. She couldn't even keep her husband interested enough at home, so he had found some slut to spend his time with. A pure hot rage swelled up inside her and she groped around the bath to turn the taps on, before immersing herself in the water to stop herself from shaking. She needed to plan what she was going to do next. If Lucas thought he was going to walk away from her without a fight, after all she had done for him, then he was sadly mistaken.

CHAPTER 21

David ambled over to where Tilly sat and crouched down in front of her, clasping her hand. She smiled at him and gave him the go-ahead to continue. He stood up and looked at the group of people in front of him. Each and every one of them was like a family member to him now.

'Okay,' he said to the expectant faces staring up at him. He wasn't quite sure when he had become the one they listened to, it had happened gradually and he was grateful for it. 'Have we decided that we will continue to let the developers poke their noses in here? We will have to be more careful of what we say. If they are starting to notice a change, then so will others. Perhaps it will be time, soon, for the world to know. But that is not our decision to make. When the time is right, we will know.'

'The newspapers reported a change and dragged us into it,' said Tilly simply. 'We were happy the way things were. But if these developers can help more children to achieve their best and give work to the wider community, then surely we have to let them in. Isn't that what we wanted from the start? To build more places like this one?' she asked David.

'Tilly's right, as usual,' he grimaced, making everyone laugh at his self-deprecating humour. 'This is such a good opportunity for the kids, both yours and ours, in the future,' he gently ran his hand over Tilly's protruding tummy. 'The world is picking up on the change of behaviour we've seen in recent years. We can't keep saying that it is just our programme that is helping them, although love and support goes a long way.'

'But we can keep them unaware for as long as possible, can't we?' said Alfie. David saw Lexi all but swoon whilst looking at his strong arms, and he bet she was wishing they were wrapped around her. Stacey gave her a sideways look, but dismissed her with a swish of her hair, making Lexi's face flame red in embarrassment at being caught mooning over someone else's boyfriend.

'We don't have to be too helpful,' said David playfully, trying to distract Lexi, 'and Tilly is right. The whole reason I started this place was to help kids turn their lives around. This way we can help more kids and create better oppor-tunities.'

'We can't risk letting more families in!' said Sarah, rising from her chair at the back. 'Surely, the more people that find out, the more chance of them messing with the new gene?'

Lucille placed a warning hand on her friend's arm, making her sit down again and blush at her outburst. David understood that Sarah was so happy there, she didn't want anyone to risk ruining it. From the look on Lucille's face, Sarah would be able to see how hypocritical she was being and she hung her head and tucked her hands in her lap.

Lucille patted her arm and quickly leant in to give her

friend a hug. David knew why Sarah didn't want outsiders in. Her life was so much happier, she didn't want it ruined by meddling. The fact that Sarah had been an outsider, before Lucille welcomed her into the fold, wasn't lost on David either.

He could see where Sarah was coming from and was sure that others felt the same, but he had started the centre to help people, not to segregate and create some sort of idealistic state. They welcomed in those who needed them and so far it had worked like a dream.

'Sorry,' mumbled Sarah, visibly shaken by her own outburst.

'It's okay to feel that you don't want your life disrupted, Sarah,' David said kindly. 'Most of us probably feel the same. But this thing is bigger than us, now, and we must find the best way to help everybody.'

Lucas walked into the lounge and sniffed the air appreciatively. 'Wow, something smells good!' he called out. He had had a long day of meetings and there had been a mix up at the golf club with a double booking, so they had needed to relocate to a nearby hotel. He had told the staff that he was really annoyed at the wasted time, but in the end it had worked out for the best as they had been shown to a plush office suite at the hotel and the golf club had ordered them a sumptuous lunch by way of an apology. 'I can't believe I'm hungry again after all that food they offered us at the meeting today, but the smell coming from the kitchen is heavenly.'

Jemima peered around the kitchen door and looked at Lucas with new eyes. Instead of seeing a downtrodden husband, she saw a man who was capable of lying to his wife and her family, a cheating scumbag who wasn't worthy of licking her boots. She had conveniently forgotten her own indiscretions; they had just been rolls in the hay. This must be serious, for Lucas to have done it, and that was just not allowed. She would bloody kill the woman who had tried to steal her husband.

She smiled sweetly at him and he frowned at the gesture. Jemima knew she had been acting so strangely of late that he didn't know what he was going to come home to next. One minute she was screaming blue murder at him, then she was being seductive and fluttering her eyelashes.

'Did the meetings go well?' she asked silkily, coming up to wind her arms around his neck and nearly garrotting him in the process. He smiled tightly and gently unwound her arms to take off his coat and shoes.

'Fine, thanks. Although we didn't get through as much of the agenda as we would have liked, as there was a hiccup in the plans,' he answered simply.

Jemima was seething inside at the lies that rolled off his tongue so easily. She would act as if nothing had happened, for now, and bide her time until she was ready to strike. Lucas wouldn't know what had hit him. He was messing with the wrong girl if he thought that she'd lie down and let some bitch come in and usurp her. Lucas was Managing Director of her father's company now, so this other woman probably thought she had hit the big time. She would certainly hit something once Jemima found out who she was. It would either be Jem's fist or a brick wall.

Jem led him into the beautifully lit dining room and he stared in awe at the opulent table, overflowing with mouth-watering delicacies. She heard his stomach rumble at the food that Sabine had cooked – for, however much she pretended, he would know without a doubt that Jemima wouldn't have got her own hands dirty by actually cooking anything. She would still tell him that the meal was of her own creation. She could lie if he could, and she'd wait to see if he went along with it. Lucas had actually tried something that she cooked once, when Sabine was off sick and they couldn't get a replacement at short notice; she had to admit that the meal had been like an assault course. First, they had had to tackle lumpy, cold mashed potato, then came the gruelling challenge of trying to pretend the charred steak was like butter in their mouths. Lucas had nearly choked on the gristle. Trying to suppress the memory, she waited for him to compliment her for the effort she had made with the table, and then took his place opposite her.

Just look at him, she fumed to herself. *He comes home as if nothing has happened.* She gritted her teeth and forced herself to smile at him. *He has lied to me and he just sits there calmly after probably spending the afternoon screwing her. Screwing both of us!* She made a silent vow to herself that she would find out who the other woman was. Her insides burned with fury and she clenched her fists and dug her nails into her palms to calm herself down. If Lucas suspected she knew what he was doing, he would remove any trace of the affair and it would look as though she was losing her marbles. She cast her mind back and now realised that there had been one or two occasions where she had questioned things he had done. He had made out that she was imagining things, and it had made her second-guess herself for a while. The absolute bastard!

Jem looked up to see Lucas studying her with a frown on his face. She quickly picked up her knife and fork and scooped a forkful of delicious creamed potato into her mouth, to stop him from asking if she was okay. It tasted like sawdust to her, but she ate it anyway, then politely enquired about his day whilst surreptitiously filling their wine glasses every time they dwindled slightly. Perhaps if he was drunk, he would talk more freely about what was happening and not remember what he had said in the morning. She was sure her father had a supply of drugs somewhere that she could use on Lucas to loosen his tongue, but she couldn't risk her father finding out what Lucas had done. Not before she had decided what to do about it herself, anyway.

CHAPTER 23

The next morning Lucas quietly groaned and held the side of his head. He must have drunk more than he realised last night. He sidled out of bed and quickly got under the shower, then grabbed his clothes and quietly left the room before Jemima woke. She had been full of seduction and sweetness last night and it had been difficult to fight her off. Only the late conference call that he had been expecting from a colleague in Japan had spared him having to push her away again. There was no way he could sleep with her now. He was in love with his delicate Poppy and the passion he had once felt for Jemima had all but disappeared. He could still look at her and appreciate her beauty, but it was only skin deep. What was inside was bitter and angry.

It was still the weekend and he had stopped telling Jem where he was going some time ago. He felt a pang of regret that his marriage hadn't worked out, but Poppy needed him now and he was going to have to find out a way of leaving Jemima whilst making her think it was her own idea.

His blood started pumping in his veins at the thought of what Teddy might do to him, but hopefully he could work out an exit plan for himself and Poppy before his father-in-law found out. He had some money stashed away. They didn't need the grandeur of the life he was leaving behind, but his child wouldn't starve. Lucas had been discreetly working on contacts that would support him in a venture of his own. Finally, he would be his own boss, but only if Teddy didn't find out first and skyrocket the whole thing.

Jem didn't know about all of Lucas's financial and business accounts, and it would be a surprise to Teddy to realise that he had underestimated the boy all along. Lucas had done Teddy's bidding for long enough. He had learnt a thing or two from Teddy and now had a network of people who could help him – at a price. Lucas had known, from the moment he met Poppy, that his life would be extremely difficult if Teddy ever found out. He had always hoped that the day wouldn't come until he could get them safely away.

They couldn't leave before the birth, as it would be too suspicious and Teddy would be alerted. Lucas's carefully laid plans wouldn't be ready by then anyway. Poppy springing the pregnancy on him had merely accelerated things. Poppy was going on maternity leave soon and, as it would be impossible for her to return to work, this had added to the weight on his shoulders. He would have to make sure she was hidden somewhere safe, then join her when the baby was a few months old. He could visit in between and no-one would be the wiser.

Feeling bad that Jem was unaware of what was about to happen to her life, Lucas hastily scribbled a note to explain that he would be out all day and not to wait up, and reached for his car keys from the rack next to the front door.

CHAPTER 24

Jem opened her eyes as soon as Lucas was in the shower and quickly pulled on jeans and a silk shirt. She hastily shoved the soft fabric into the waist of her jeans and then leaped back into bed, pulling the covers up to her chin and feigning sleep as Lucas crept through the bedroom and out of the door. By the time he was getting into his car, she was racing down the stairs and grabbing her own keys.

She pulled her car out of the driveway as soon as Lucas had turned left on to the main road, and slowly followed him to his destination. He was so wrapped up in what he was doing that he didn't even notice her bright red sports car following a short way behind. Lucas had managed to untangle himself from her arms and take his business call last night, which had strangely taken hours to complete. She had waited for as long as she could for him to come to bed, but had eventually fallen into a disturbed sleep.

When she had felt him leave the bed this morning, she had been instantly awake. No man was allowed to make a fool of her. Without thinking, she had dressed and decided to follow him, wherever he was going.

Jemima blinked away tears as she saw Lucas's car slow and turn into a large apartment block. It looked very unassuming and the uniform flats sitting side by side were functional and not at all pretty. *What on earth was Lucas doing here?* she wondered. His car pulled into a designated parking space and Jemima swung her sports car across the road and into a supermarket car park.

Her heart racing, she quickly slammed the door and ignored the curious glances from a young family loading their weekly food shop into the boot of their car. Darting a look left and right Jemima ran across the road, but Lucas was nowhere to be seen. She trailed around the car park until she found his car. The parking space had a flat number on it – 212. There was another car parked in the next space along, both for the same flat. The other car was newish, but a dark blue and Jem had no idea what make it was. It looked boring and solid and the headlights seemed to be staring at her, mocking her for being there.

She wanted to scratch deep indents into both cars and then go and hammer on the door to find them in there together, but knew this wasn't the right time. She would have to come back when Lucas wasn't here, and find out what she was up against then.

Later that evening, Jemima heard Lucas come into the house and didn't even bother to look up. If he was surprised to not have her bounce over and fling her arms around him, he didn't show it and he went and sat in the chair opposite her.

'How has your day been, Jem?' he asked gently, and she wondered if he was feeling like a heel for spending the day with another woman, and if he was having trouble juggling any feelings he still had for her, now he was involved with this nameless bitch.

Jemima caught him by surprise by simply smiling up at him then pretending to be engrossed in the novel grasped in her hand. 'Fine, thanks,' she said through gritted teeth, keeping her tone as light as she could manage and controlling the urge to jump up and slap his cheating face.

'Dinner is keeping warm in the oven if you want some.' She stretched her arms above her head, giving him an eyeful of perfect breast under her sheer blouse. Then she leant down to place her book on the side table.

'You going out?' said Lucas, looking confused at Jem's behaviour and the fact that she seemed to be going somewhere, as she had got up and was putting a short gilet on over her soft mauve shirt.

'I'm going for a quick drink with one of my girlfriends,' she called casually over her shoulder. 'You want to join us?'

Lucas frowned as Jem never went out to meet a girlfriend on a weekend. She bit her lip to stop herself from screaming at him that she was finally starting to make a new life for herself. He should be glad of this, as it would make his life easier, but she couldn't help the feeling of loss at the change in their marriage. He was so used to the arguments and stress every day that he didn't know how to respond to a wife that left him alone. He was probably wondering what he was supposed to do with his evening now, as he could have stayed longer with that woman. Well, now he could stay home alone and see what that felt like.

She wondered if he had, in the past, felt that Jem might be seeing other men, but he'd not brought it up and it was certainly nothing he would ever be able to prove. She was always saying how boring he was and how she was never allowed to have fun, so it could hardly surprise him if she had sought comfort elsewhere. She wondered how he would feel if he had evidence that she had been sleeping with another man, if he would feel jealous at the thought of someone else touching her. However hypocritical this was, she was still his wife. She abhorred the thought of him with another woman and she certainly wouldn't just sit back and let it happen.

'I'm tired now,' Lucas stated to Jem's retreating back. 'I think I will just catch up on some paperwork for tomorrow and have an early night. Have fun!'

As if, thought Jem, as she once again reached for her car keys and followed the route she had taken earlier that day.

CHAPTER 25

David and Tilly sat on the sofa, in their colourful lounge, arms and legs sprawled all over each other. David kept tickling Tilly's feet and making her giggle like mad, but he had her legs pinned under his and she couldn't escape. 'Let me go!' she gasped, pleading with him. 'You might bring on the baby!'

David stopped immediately and Tilly laughed at his worried expression. 'It's not due for a few weeks yet, you dope!'

He relaxed his hold on her and bent down to kiss her toes, making her squeal again and she got up into a sitting position next to him. 'We need to talk about what's happening on the development site,' she said, quite serious now.

'I know,' he soothed, 'but I don't want you to be stressed by anything, especially as this is your last trimester with the baby.'

'David,' she giggled, 'I love the fact that you are so protective of me and our baby, but I am a big girl and I can take a few serious discussions about a business that we now both run together.'

'I think there is something fishy going on with the developers,' said David thoughtfully. 'Dr Cole has admitted that MAZE is the parent company. I know he said that there are many subsidiaries, but my contact tells me that Teddy Venner has his fingers in everything that matters. Why do we matter? The only reason they would be bothering with us is because of the low birth rate. Someone has found out something about why it's happening and that, for some reason, has put us in their path.' David gently rubbed Tilly's shoulders but she winced as he was pressing too hard. 'Sorry,' he said, realising he was pummelling, rather than relaxing, her tight muscles. This must be affecting her more than she was saying, judging by how rigid her shoulders were.

'But who would have told them?' questioned Tilly, with a frown on her lovely face. 'Do you think someone would have exposed us, for money?'

'No!' said David jumping up and pacing the room, back and forth, back and forth, until Tilly stood up and put out a hand to steady him. He glanced at her hand as if in a daze, then shook himself and re-focused. 'Everyone on the estate has too much to lose if anyone interferes. Parents lose childcare and a way for the kids to let off steam, and the kids would lose a safe place to go and someone to look out for them. There are loads of people on the estate who don't know what we are doing, but they have learnt to turn a blind eye. The same way they expect us to leave them to their business and not stick our noses where they are not wanted. It's worked so far.'

'But what if they've finally managed to get one of our kids on to drugs, or have blackmailed or threatened them?'

she worried, smoothing and re-smoothing a small crease in her green maternity top.

'We would know about it, Tills,' he said, looking her straight in the eye and leading her back to the couch to sit down. He didn't like the flush that had come into her cheeks. He quickly went to their small kitchen and filled a glass with cold water for her.

'There would have been signs that someone was using. Their behaviour would have been different and someone else would have told us about it. We are too tight a community to let that pass by unnoticed now. The drug pushers know to leave us alone and they wouldn't touch one of our kids. They know we would cause all kinds of trouble for them in return. If any of our families were desperate for money, they would come to us first. They understand how the bartering system works. We can use it for almost anything. We're so careful about who we tell, Tills. No one else knows anything.'

'You think it's a coincidence they chose us?' she asked.

'No. But I don't think their information came from us. I think they have their own network and we just happen to be useful to them in some other way. Perhaps they've found out the real reason why people can't have children and we're wrong about it.'

Tilly ran her fingers over his hand. 'You know you are not wrong. We've seen it for ourselves. Perhaps it was just the story in the paper that brought them here?'

'It was a story about the kids' performance, not about how many babies are being born, but they are definitely interested in you and the other pregnant women, not just that we do get results from the kids. I'm happy to share the knowledge about how we help children achieve amazing results, if it helps other children to fulfil their dreams. We are just giving them love and support, finding what they are naturally good at and training them properly.'

'It's obviously possible for kids from all walks of life to do well. If they have talent, it doesn't matter if they come from an estate or a castle. All we do is spot the talent and nurture it. It's not rocket science,' he said. 'If these guys want to build up the area, provide us with more work and think we are providing them with a service for our time, then more fool them. I would have happily told anyone all that anyway, if they had bothered to ask the right questions.' He rubbed his temples and rolled his own shoulders backwards. 'There are kids all over the world that are born with talent, there just aren't many places like this that find them and help them reach their potential.'

Tilly sighed deeply, suddenly looking tired now. He guessed she was worried about bringing Dr Cole amongst them if he wasn't genuine, even though she was convinced that he was one of the good guys. 'There must be children everywhere that have gifts in so many areas who never get an opportunity to use them, just like you nearly didn't. Your family tried to squash any hope you had of being gifted at something. You just want to help kids find out what they can achieve and have a chance to show others.'

David got up and offered Tilly a hand. 'Come on. I'll run you a warm bubbly bath and bring you a glass of lemonade. I might even order a takeaway so we don't have to cook!' Tilly smiled and kissed his nose. He hated to see her so upset and knew she felt guilty at the part she had played in bringing the developers into their lives. If only they hadn't agreed to that news story in the first place.

CHAPTER 26

Tilly pulled on a soft, moss coloured, cable knit jumper and sighed in contentment. The bath had been heavenly and had helped to ease some of the tension she had been carrying around for days now. She felt bad that MAZE was doing something underhand, but surely if they were going to cause trouble, they would have done it by now? Dr Cole was being so solicitous and kind to her. She usually felt a lot calmer having him around. She hadn't told David, but she had had one or two light bleeds. She knew that David would worry and the hospitals around here were full to capacity. They couldn't afford private health care. Having Dr Cole's soothing presence and asking his advice had been a double-edged sword. Firstly, she shouldn't have lied to David and secondly, the lies were getting worse. Dr Cole had realised something was wrong and had found her quietly weeping one morning in the office at the warehouse. He had offered to examine her at his medical facility and she had felt the weight of the world being lifted from her shoulders. The problem was that she still hadn't plucked up the courage to tell David. He would be mad at her for not involving him, and for confiding in Dr Cole before him. Part of the deal for having the developers around had been for Dr Cole to keep an eye on her anyway, although she knew deep down that David had just been protecting her as usual and hadn't expected there to be any need for emergency medical advice. She straightened her back and decided that she would tell David tonight. Dr Cole had taken blood samples and said she had nothing to worry about. There had been no more blood loss, so she was sure he was right. She was also convinced that they were wrong about Dr Cole. He seemed genuine to her. No one could be that good an actor, surely?

The doorbell buzzed and Tilly went to open it. She was completely astounded to find Alfie standing beside a sheepish-looking Lexi. Tilly raised her eyebrows at Alfie, but his friend just shrugged and followed her into the lounge, flopping down on the nearest chair.

'Oh! Hi, Lexi,' said David, surprise in his voice at seeing Lexi in their home. Tilly knew that Lexi had a huge crush on Alfie and she was cross at him for leading the poor girl on. What on earth was he thinking of, bringing her here? Stacey would have a fit! Tilly thought of her friend and knew that she would *not* be happy when she heard they'd come over. She would also, more than likely, blame Tilly. Stacey wasn't the most reasonable person at the best of times, but Tilly loved her anyway. She was a loyal friend and she clearly adored Alfie. *What was Alfie playing at?*

David grabbed Alfie a beer and a lemonade for Tilly and Lexi. Tilly gave him a worried frown, she had a bad feeling about this. Lexi really didn't like Stacey and she wasn't grown up enough yet not to tell Stacey she had been round with Alfie, just to wind her up. Stacey would go mad! With the position they were in with the MAZE group, Tilly and David couldn't risk even one person being upset right now. They'd known Alfie a very long time, and understood Lexi was just a friend – but did Lexi know that?

Alfie grinned and obviously decided to put them out of their misery, but looked like he'd thoroughly enjoyed winding them up for a moment. 'Everyone's so serious these days,' he joked. 'Lexi offered to bake something nice for you, Tilly, as you need a bit of tender loving care at the moment,' he winked at Tilly and she visibly relaxed. It took David a moment or two longer, as he seemed annoyed at Alfie for playing a joke on them at Lexi's expense. 'So I offered to carry them to your flat as I was coming anyway. Plus, I thought I might get to eat one of Lexi's amazing cakes if I brought them for her,' he winked at Lexi as if she was his co-conspirator.

Tilly smiled kindly at Lexi, who was blushing now. She walked over to the huge plate of cupcakes on the side table and offered one to everybody. 'I just wanted to check that you and the baby were okay?' Lexi said.

'Why wouldn't she be?' parried David, through a mouthful of delectable iced cake.

'Oh!' stammered Lexi, back-peddling fast at the stricken look on Tilly's face and the question on David's. 'I just thought that Tilly was doing too much and wanted to cheer her up.'

'Are you doing too much?' growled David, staring at Tilly with suddenly fierce eyes.

Tilly sent Lexi a glance and tried to soothe David. Lexi must have overheard her talking to Dr Cole about the bleeding. That girl knew far too much sometimes, but she was so quiet on her feet, that you hardly ever knew she was there. Tilly would have to tell David now, before Lexi did, although it seemed the girl had realised she had put her foot in it. She would now be wondering why Tilly hadn't told David about the blood loss, and that was just what Tilly needed!

'I'm fine,' she laughed, patting his hand in a motherly fashion, hopefully confusing him all the more.

If he suspected she was lying to him, he would make sure he found out what it was about, one way or another. He was astute enough to realise Tilly was worrying about something and Lexi, of all people, knew exactly what it was.

What would they do if someone told Dr Cole something out of pique, too? The way Lexi was observing Alfie from under her lashes, whilst he was regaling David with some quip or other, made Tilly cringe. Poor Lexi was on a hiding to nothing with her obsession. Things were starting to get complicated and Tilly would have to sort this mess out quickly before it escalated and changed all of their lives forever.

CHAPTER 27

Jem pulled into the same supermarket car park she had used earlier, across the street from the block of flats that Lucas had visited. She sat in her car trying to calm her breathing. She didn't know what she was going to do next, but she did know that she wasn't going to sit there for much longer, while some bitch was metres away from her, thinking that Lucas was now her property. She would soon learn her mistake, and wish she had never been born! Jem would find a way to make her pay for what she'd done. She didn't need her dad to do her dirty work for her. She was her father's daughter and a glint of steel came into her eyes. She straightened her back, got out of the car and crossed the street to find out what sort of enemy she was facing.

As she looked at the numbers of the flats, a young man passing by gave Jemima the once over, smiling her way and trying to catch her eye. Jem ignored his blatant staring. She was used to this sort of attention from men of all ages. She carried on until she was outside flat number 212. She could faintly hear a television and someone singing from behind another door, and took another deep breath to steady herself.

Just as Jem was about to knock at the door, it flew open. Poppy stood before her, shopping bag and purse in her hand, and a dumbstruck expression on her face. Jem just stared at Poppy. How stupid of her! She must have got this wrong. Lucas must just have been dropping off documents for work. She started backing away, but then she noticed Poppy's heavily protruding stomach.

Poppy looked down at her belly, too, and all colour drained from her face. Jemima stared at her incredulously. This couldn't be right. Poppy was so dull, and not even very pretty. It must be a mistake, but from the look on Poppy's ashen face, Jemima knew that she had inadvertently knocked at the door of one of her biggest fears. Not only had Lucas been sleeping with someone else, but she was stuffed full of his child. And he would only screw someone this dowdy if he loved her.

Jemima shoved her way into the flat, almost knocking Poppy over. She frantically grabbed the radiator for support. Jemima slammed the door shut before her adversary could run out of it, and screamed in Poppy's face. 'Get into the lounge, you jumped-up little bitch! How dare you sleep with my husband? You think that he won't get bored with a dumpy little mouse like you? Well, I'm telling you now that he will.'

Poppy flung herself into one of her soft armchairs, shifting to accommodate the weight of her heavily pregnant stomach. Tears ran down her face and she frantically scrubbed them away, so that Jemima wouldn't see her cry, but it was too late. 'I'm so ashamed of what I've done with Lucas,' she sobbed. 'You have every right to hate and revile me. I've stolen your husband.' Poppy pushed herself back up off the chair and ran into her tiny bathroom to be sick.

Jem watched Poppy's retreating form and almost felt sorry for her... almost! Lucas must have gone all-out to get a dried up old prune like Poppy into bed. The poor girl had probably never even had sex before, and now here she was, up the duff by some man who wasn't her husband. Jemima snarled at the door to the bathroom and hoped Poppy was feeling as bad as she deserved for what she had done. The fact that she was pregnant was the final straw for Jemima.

Poppy came back from the bathroom looking slightly better than she had gone in, but only just. *She does have a spark of defiance in her eye now, though*, thought Jem with interest. Perhaps the girl had some spunk after all?

'What do you care what Lucas does anyway?' asked Poppy groggily, groping round for something to hold on to and sinking once again into the nearest chair. 'You hardly give him the time of day. Do you really care if he's seeing someone else?' Poppy sounded like she really did want to know. 'The way you treat him makes me cringe. A man as sensitive as Lucas can only take so much.' Jemima knew mousy Poppy had seen her in action, shouting at Lucas and emasculating him.

Jem's eyes narrowed and she saw Poppy flinch as she looked up and saw the pure hatred in them. Poppy began to stumble over her words. 'I feel so bad that I have feelings for Lucas... but I'm sure I wouldn't have gone near him if you were nicer to him.' She seemed surprised that Jemima was so angry with her. 'I always assumed that you didn't care what Lucas did.' Fear burned in her eyes when Jem walked towards her and she held her arms over her stomach protectively.

'You don't think that I would care that my husband is

screwing his secretary?' she spat. 'Talk about being a walking cliché! What is the matter with you, Poppy? Are you so pitiful that you can't find a man of your own? You have to steal someone else's when they're vulnerable?' Jemima said contemptuously.

'Lucas isn't vulnerable,' whispered Poppy, looking frantically past Jemima for a way out of her own home.

'Oh, you know him so well, do you?' shrieked Jemima. 'How long has this sordid affair been going on?' gesturing to Poppy's stomach. 'Obviously at least nine months.'

'I'm so sorry for what I've done,' cried Poppy. 'I hate myself, but I love Lucas and he loves me.'

Jemima felt like she had been cut by a knife and she bent over and gasped for air. How could Lucas love this insipid girl, when he had a vivacious butterfly like her at home?

'As you are fully aware,' said Jemima brokenly, trying to regain her composure. 'Lucas and I have been trying for a baby for some time, and this puts a lot of strain on a relationship. We make love all the time,' she felt a shard of victory when this little gem hit home, even though it wasn't true. Poppy's face crumpled and she started to weep quietly.

'You thought he wasn't sleeping with me? Oh, poor Poppy. We've always gone at it like wild cats. Why do you think we fight? Lucas loves the making up at night when he gets home,' she said, casting a sly glance at her rival.

Jemima pulled out a footstool and brought it to sit right in front of Poppy, making the girl shrink back into her seat. 'Here's how this thing is going to play out, Poppy,' she said. 'That baby is going to be mine now.' Jemima was quite enjoying the look of pure horror in Poppy's eyes. She hoped the girl was suffering for what she had done. 'You will tell Lucas you have lost the baby in childbirth. I will say I am looking into adoption and have the prospect of a baby.'

'No way,' shouted Poppy, jumping up and knocking into Jemima as she passed. She ran to the kitchen and backed up against the counter. 'When it comes to my baby, you'll soon learn about a mother's instinct to protect her child,' she said. 'There's no way I'm was going to give a madwoman like you my firstborn.' Opening a drawer, she felt around for a large carving knife, and frantically dropped it on the work surface behind her.

Jemima followed Poppy into the kitchen and eyed her warily. Poppy's manic look made Jem think she was going to bolt, but she would be going nowhere until she had agreed to do as she had been told.

'Think about it,' said Jem. 'Your baby will still be with its biological father, even if he doesn't know it, and you will be saving both Lucas's and the baby's life.'

Poppy stared at the monster in front of her and felt along the kitchen counter for the knife. She ran her fingers along the handle and grasped it in her hand behind her back.

'What do you mean, saving both their lives?'

'Have you met my father?' asked Jemima menacingly, blocking the kitchen doorway.

'Yes,' whispered Poppy.

'Maybe you don't know him so well, but if he finds out that his daughter's husband has been screwing the staff, then said husband will probably find his baby-maker cut off and the staff member will wake up to find themselves half way down a cliff face in the middle of nowhere.'

Poppy moved away from Jem and held the knife out in front of her, shaking violently.

Jemima looked at her dispassionately. 'You think you

can survive this, Poppy? Well, you can't. You picked the wrong family to play with and now your fingers are quite literally about to be burnt. Think about what I have said. You don't really have a lot of options. Play it my way or all of you can end up in a ditch. The choice is yours.'

With that, Jemima calmly turned and walked back out the way she had come, pausing in the now empty communal hallway, where she promptly threw up in the corner. She hated Lucas now with every fibre of her being. She would make him suffer for what he had done to her. Ruining his relationship with Poppy and getting him to bring up his own child without knowing it would be enough for now, but once everything was settled, she would make him suffer all over again. Jemima felt a ring of steel go around her heart and ice fill her veins. She'd thought that Lucas had once brought out a slightly softer side in her, but she would never forget this pain. He was going to regret playing her for a fool, and she would make him continue to pay every day for the rest of his miserable life. She would almost have been amused, if she hadn't felt so cold. All the times she had craved her father's attention, and this was probably the one moment when he would have been proud of her.

CHAPTER 28

Poppy tried to scrunch herself into a tiny ball on her couch, but her stomach prevented her, which made her sob harder still. She wished she had never got herself into such a mess, but knew that she would always have been too weak to resist a man like Lucas. Perhaps this was punishment for what she had done. A man like him would never normally take an interest in a girl like her. He wasn't really what you would class as Alpha male, but he was still commanding, and knew how to get exactly what he wanted. He had got her pregnant after all.

She thought about phoning him, but what could he say? Supposing they really were in danger from Jemima's father? If she told Lucas about what was happening to her, then he would help her, surely? But if it meant putting his life in danger, how could she tell him?

She picked up her phone to call him, then put it down again, sobbing louder now. She couldn't turn to her family for help, either. She had been unable to tell them the news, knowing they would disown her and revile her for being an unwed mother. How could she explain to them that she had got pregnant by another woman's husband? The shame of it would kill her mother. She'd always deferred to Poppy's father, a studious, quiet man who had very old-fashioned views on the world. He would ask her to leave and never return. The thought of her sweet mother never speaking to her again made Poppy drag herself into her bedroom and bury herself under the covers, until she had no more tears to cry.

Her relationship with her parents was usually quite good, but Poppy had always known that they were both reserved and liked a quiet life, as did Poppy. They had tried to persuade her out of a city job, claiming that the small town they lived in was more than enough excitement for a girl like her, but she hadn't listened to them. She'd thought that she'd known best and that the city might help her to make friends and be more confident. How wrong could she have been? No-one at work or in her block of flats even gave her the time of day, except for Lucas.

Lucas had not only paid her attention, but actively sought out her opinion and cared about what she thought from day one. She had been like a forlorn puppy waiting for someone to show it affection. She could see that now. She really did feel in her heart that he loved her, whatever Jemima had thrown at her. The thought of them making love together, though, made her feel physically sick. Had Lucas lied to her and been sleeping with them both all along?

She needed to clear her head. *I have someone else to think about now,* she thought, stroking her belly and trying to soothe both herself and her baby. Keeping them all alive was her main priority. She could run, but where would she hide? If Jemima's father was as ruthless as both Lucas and Jemima had said he was, then she would never be able to run far enough.

CHAPTER 29

Teddy really wanted to hurt somebody. He didn't even really care who it was. He hadn't felt like this in a long time, as he ran his business in such a way that he didn't need to. People knew what he was capable of and that was usually enough to keep them in line. He wouldn't tolerate stress, and the respectable façade he had built up as a reputable businessman was at risk if anyone saw him lose control.

The way Lucas had treated Jemima was almost enough to remind him of how he used to do business in the old days. He hadn't had a team of people working for him then. Everything he had created had been of his own making. Every bone that cracked had been broken by his own hands. Today, Teddy wanted to get his hands dirty again, but he knew he couldn't risk getting involved personally, or his carefully constructed empire could fall down like a house of cards.

He scrutinised the photo of Jemima and Lucas smiling out from a solid silver frame on his desk, and wondered at what point Lucas had gotten greedy. Teddy had seen the girl in his office, scampering about. She was pretty enough, with piercing blue eyes, but was unremarkable otherwise. Teddy could understand a quick roll in the hay, maybe even turn a blind eye to that, but getting her pregnant was just plain stupid. Especially when it seemed that Jemima had finally decided to start a family of her own. Teddy was sure there couldn't be anything wrong with her, and Lucas could obviously sire a child, so it must have been stress that was stopping Jemima getting pregnant. Finding out about Lucas's infidelity would only make matters worse for her. There was no way a child of Teddy's would be infertile, so it couldn't be anything to do with Jemima. Perhaps Lucas had not been paying her enough attention and the stress of trying for a baby had overwhelmed her. He knew that this could affect the chances of reproducing.

Teddy slammed the picture face down on his desk, startling his PA, Susie, who was at her workstation outside his office. You could normally hear a pin drop in the corridors. No-one stood around chatting and there were only a few of them on the executive levels of the exquisitely designed building. Teddy usually had his door open unless he was on the phone, but he was often out of the office anyway. Susie looked up, but he waved her away, so she bent her head and once again began arranging his diary for the following week.

Teddy walked over to his office door and gently pushed it closed, which was quite a feat considering how angry he felt. He didn't want to make Susie come into the office, as she had never seen him upset before. She would panic and try and resolve the problem for him, as that was what he paid her very highly to do. No, he had decided how he would handle this little matter, and now he would sort it out himself.

He moved back behind his desk and opened his top drawer. Taking a bottle of pills from their hiding place and placing two on his palm, he threw them into his mouth and followed them with a swift gulp of the whisky that was sitting in a crystal glass on his desk.

The benefits of owning a pharmaceutical company was that he could take whatever he liked. These were tablets that kept him looking young with his mind alert, but he also had vials of powder for when he needed a different kind of pleasure. He knew that drugs could fry his brain cells, but he was pretty sure he took enough supplements to counterbalance the effects, or at least some of them. He had regular injections into his face which kept him looking youthful and strong, but his bones often ached now when he played tennis and he couldn't hide the way the skin had begun to sag around his eyes this week, with the extra stress he was under. Once he had rectified the problem with fertility, he would give himself an overhaul at one of his clinics and come back looking better than ever.

Tapping a vial of white powder onto the back of his hand, he snorted it quickly and brushed his nose to hide any remnants of the drug. Steadying himself in his chair for a moment, he closed his eyes and felt the adrenaline race through his system. When he opened his eyes, they were filled with a new fire to get the job done.

CHAPTER 30

Dr Cole picked up the receiver and listened to the instructions given to him. He didn't know what this girl, Poppy, had done to deserve the wrath of Mr Venner, but it must have been pretty bad to warrant him taking an interest in her. Dr Cole rubbed his hands in anticipation. Another baby was about to fall straight into his lap. He desperately wanted to get hold of Tilly's baby. He didn't know why, but he felt that this particular child would answer some of the questions he had about the mutating gene. He didn't know if the mutation had been passed from parent to child to cause later infertility, or if there was an environmental factor involved. Maybe something was causing radiation somewhere, although this might rule out anything being passed on to the next generation. The only way to tell if the babies had the same gene was to test them.

He had Tilly in his grasp now, but the problem was David. It had been his idea to let Dr Cole look at Tilly in the first place. He had played right into Dr Cole's hands by asking him to supervise her medical care at the clinic. She was used to popping in every few days since she had had her first blood loss, and hadn't asked why he was doing so many tests on her and the baby. She assumed he was helping her and making sure she didn't miscarry. She had been so frightened at the first slight blood loss it had been easy to get her to cooperate. He would do everything in his power to save this child, as he needed it to test his theories on. The blood loss had not endangered the baby, but he hadn't told Tilly that, just that he would need regular blood samples to make sure the baby was safe. He hadn't even had to cause the blood loss himself. It was as if someone was finally looking out for him and the stars in his sky had aligned.

He was desperate to find something in the blood samples to save him from further testing on the baby when it was born, but things weren't looking good. He was hoping to see changes to the cells, which would tell him he was on the right path. It hadn't happened. He had even considered inducing Tilly's labour early to find out what was going on here. None of the other women from the warehouse had given birth yet, either. It was like a planned event. He was getting so frustrated. He couldn't go around offering to see all of the women, or he would arouse suspicion. He could probably slip one of them something to bring on labour, but it was too risky. He would ruin all his hard work if he messed up now.

Tilly was the one he really wanted, anyway. Now this new girl, Poppy – though her baby would prove whether there was something special about David and Tilly's child after all. He would test them both. He was sure they were hiding something, but he had only found technical data so far from EVE. There was a definite rise in the levels of accomplishment in children from the centre, but they wouldn't agree to blood tests, so he couldn't rule out substance abuse. Perhaps it was some sort of cult where they were all made to take steroids and had to get sponsorship to bring in money. Though who knew where all that money went? The place was pretty run down, by Dr Cole's standards. If they had money, surely they would buy better equipment and have bigger houses?

He would have to get Tilly in and start doing a few more invasive tests. He just needed to find a way to explain why he was doing it, whilst making her feel even more grateful than she already did to him for helping her. He was sure she hadn't told David about her visits to him either, which was interesting. Perhaps he would have to use his original idea to make her ill, then cure her. He would have to tread gently with this one, but her due date was looming and Dr Cole couldn't help the fear and excitement he felt at maybe solving the puzzle that had been plaguing him for years.

CHAPTER 31

David walked through the streets that surrounded the warehouse. It was the same view every way you looked; dust, grime and poverty. The warehouse seemed to rise up out of the barren landscape and stand tall amongst the rubble. There were hardly any plants growing and even the few cars dotted around seemed to be covered in a thin sheen of fog. He idly kicked a stone as he walked towards EVE and wondered why the thought of the developers bringing employment and facilities worried him so much.

Dr Cole had been really courteous to Tilly and she was much calmer for having him around. *Perhaps I'm jealous,* thought David with a self-deprecating grin. *Jealous of an old man because he's helping my girlfriend where I can't. How ridiculous! Maybe I need to start welcoming the developers and actually helping them, like I promised, rather than staying out of their way and letting them get on with their research?* After all, he surmised, it was the kids turning their lives around that had interested them in the first place, and that was his idea. Maybe the developers had seen Tilly was pregnant in that newspaper article and sent Dr Cole to coax them into helping? But the developers had bought the site now, so what more did they need?

He straightened his shoulders and decided that if he wanted these guys out of his hair, then he would have to start co-operating. After all, they seemed to be keeping up their end of the bargain for the intrusion. So far, several children had been given gym membership for training at their nearest sporting village, which was in the city centre. Only the best of the athletes had been selected, though. Lucille had also been over to see the development's crèche facilities, to give them the benefit of her experience and discuss the needs of children in this area. The crèche they were building in the local sports centre was amazing, and Lucille was all but glowing with pride. It had only been a matter of weeks, but as the plans had already been provisionally agreed and the building works had been half completed before the last company went belly up, as soon as they got the green light, they had forged ahead at an amazing speed. These guys were certainly following through on their promises, and the locals were keeping to theirs. People were actually starting to apply for jobs on the sporting site and some of EVE's parents were now working there, helping with the building development and site management.

David was really pleased about this, but did worry that their loyalty would now be with the developers and not him. It was a very clever game that these people were playing, and it was so subtle that if you blinked you might miss it. If David hadn't lived the life he had, then the subtleties might have eluded him too, but he felt the undercurrent when Dr Cole was around and just knew that they were being played. David had his ear to the ground and he knew some of the EVE parents had been offered extra perks that other workers had not. The developers obviously thought it would keep them onside and earn their gratitude, as they had never had benefits like this from an employer before.

What they didn't realise was that the EVE parents were a close community who told David everything. Many of them ran their employment contracts past David and Tilly first, as none of them had been in jobs like this previously, even before the area became so rundown. David was also smart enough to go and make himself known to the workers they already had on board. Many of them were the usual team of builders that MAZE employed, and David was careful to enquire what they were like to work for, pretending that he might be looking for a new job. The upshot was that none of the regular employees got any perks, and he was as sure as hell that they would be mightily upset if anyone ever told them that the newbies were coining it in. David was pretty confident that he could even the playing field if MAZE tried anything with the EVE parents. If they did, he would fight back. For now, he had told people to enjoy the perks and to keep quiet about them. If anyone from MAZE asked more questions, then they were to act dumb. MAZE assumed they were playing with these men and women, but they had kept their secret for years, and MAZE was underestimating them if they thought a few treats would sway them.

I don't know what Alfie was playing at either, David thought with concern, *bringing Lexi over to their house the other night.* Lexi was a sweet kid, but she had had problems of her own. She had been determined to cause trouble for her grandparents until Lucille had bumped into them. Lucille had told David that she had overheard the way Lexi was speaking to her grandmother and realised that the rebellion she heard in Lexi's voice was born of boredom and frustration. Lucille had watched them arguing in the road by the little supermarket and had pretended to drop her shopping at her feet.

Lexi hadn't offered to help, but her grandad had. Lucille thanked him for his help, then cheekily explained that there was a great warehouse centre round the corner for children Lexi's age. Lexi's grandad was at the end of his tether with his wild grandchild and gratefully wrote the address down.

Lexi had turned out to be a real asset to EVE and her baking skills were sublime, but David knew that her crush on Alfie was getting worse by the minute. Most of the girls who were all over Alfie knew that he wasn't interested. Lexi, though, seemed to think that one day all her dreams would come true. Alfie would suddenly realise that Stacey was not the girl for him and would turn his attention to Lexi.

David knew this was a lost cause, as his friend had taken years of wooing to finally get Stacey to go out with him. His friend had got it bad. For all his flirting and wily ways with the ladies, he was strictly a one-woman man once he had got his girl. Stacey might drive David mad sometimes with her primping and spoilt ways, but she seemed to love Alfie as much as he loved her. David hoped that Lexi wasn't about to throw a spanner in the works. Alfie might profess to love Stacey, but if Lexi had set her sights on him, then heaven help him.

CHAPTER 32

Lucas broke off from the discussion he was having in one of MAZE's meeting rooms and frowned when he saw Poppy scurrying past. He had barely seen her this week and every time he tried to call her or reach out to her, she mumbled something about having to be somewhere else and rushed away. He had been so overrun with plans for the new sporting village that his group were building on a huge disused site outside town that he had barely a free moment to question her about it. Suddenly, Teddy had been querying every move he made and the workload was piling up.

He'd been running sites like this for years and his team covered everything, from getting the best architect right down to which sporting personality would be a favourable match to promote it, and what range of their health supplementary products would sell in the targeted area. They had found over the years that each town needed a different approach, and they did extensive research on every separate location to make sure that the brand matched the customer. Otherwise, they would be out of pocket and the whole project would be a waste of time. What worked in one part of the world would not necessarily have the same result in a place where people had different needs to be met.

This latest project was in a rundown area, which was just begging for a cash injection. Many of the locals were unemployed. If MAZE provided them with an income for working on the build or in their stores and gyms, there was nowhere else around for them to spend their hard-earned cash. It also meant that the company got loyalty from the surrounding areas for being a good employer. Then the money would start rolling in. Once the big boys bought a piece of retail space, then lots of smaller businesses always followed. Soon the area would be buzzing with new homes and designer stores, and the sporting village would be at the heart of it all.

'Ladies, gentlemen,' said Lucas, standing up and extending his hand for them to shake. 'I think that concludes our business for today, don't you?' He was desperate to find Poppy and see if she really had been avoiding him. His gut twisted at the thought of what might be wrong. He hoped there was nothing amiss with her or their baby.

'The build seems to be on track and we've managed to get the lower levels in place,' said one of the men close to Lucas, as he shook his hand and moved to the door. 'It shouldn't be too long before the second level goes in and we can make everything watertight. The original builders made a bit of a mess of things, but at least the main structure was sound. Our team are smashing through the work like a whirlwind. It's amazing what they've achieved already.'

Lucas was barely listening and politely ushered the assembled men and women out of the door, walking briskly to reception with them and chatting amiably, whilst directing them towards the exit as fast as he could without appearing impolite. This was a team that he had hand-picked to get this project off the ground, and they really were doing a good job at following his exacting standards. Lucas was a perfectionist and never left the slightest nuance to chance, so he needed to be concentrating now, but he just couldn't shake the niggling feeling that something wasn't right. He usually signed off the final labour costs too, but the accounts office informed him that this had already been done. He would have to look into it when he found a spare minute in his punishing schedule.

As soon as he had bade his farewells, he rapidly turned and slammed his hand against the button for the lift, tapping his foot impatiently while he waited for it to return to the ground floor. Every floor that lit up on the screen seemed to take forever and when the doors finally sprung open, he was into the lift and sending it back up to the executive suite before it had had a chance to open fully.

Poppy wouldn't be expecting anyone, as she thought that Lucas was in an important conference and would be busy for hours yet. The planning meeting usually dragged on for ages with Lucas picking over the minutest detail. He knew he was a hard taskmaster, but he always got the job done. The reception desk normally filtered visitors wanting to come up to these offices, so she normally wouldn't be bothered by anyone.

Poppy gasped when the lift doors slid open and she saw Lucas. He took her arm and marched her gently into his office, when he saw how pale and frightened she looked. He closed the door behind them and pulled out a chair for her.

Crouching down in front of her, he said, 'Poppy, what on earth is going on? Are you all right? Is the baby okay?' She was starting to scare him.

'I can't do this any more, Lucas,' she sobbed, wringing her hands together nervously.

Lucas hoped no one was looking and pulled her into his arms while she wept on his shoulder. He led her into the opulent washroom that adjoined his office and leaned her against the side of the sink. At least in here they were away from prying eyes. Not that there seemed to be anyone else around today, which was strange. There were usually a handful of people working diligently at their desks in the offices next door. Then he remembered that they were all on the lower floor at a training seminar.

'Can't do what?' he soothed, stroking her hair out of her eyes and gently kissing away her tears.

'I can't give up my baby. I only dared to come into work because I knew that you had a really busy schedule this week and that you probably wouldn't have time to see me anyway.'

'Poppy!' he scolded, being firmer with her than he intended, but needing to get her attention. 'What on earth are you talking about? Why would you have to give up our baby? Is there something wrong with it?' A feeling of dread filled his body and he almost shook her to make her answer him.

'Jemima knows about us,' she gasped, her face contorting in pain.

'What?' cried Lucas incredulously. 'How could Jem have found out? Have you seen her?' he half-accused.

He flinched as Poppy winced in pain again and bent over. 'She followed you to my house. She threatened to take away our baby and keep it for herself. She said her father would kill you,' said Poppy through gritted teeth, tears streaming unchecked down her face now.

All the colour drained from Lucas's face as he pulled

the sobbing Poppy into his arms. She buried her face in his chest, gasping for air between muffled wails. 'I thought I was strong enough to fight her and protect my baby, but she's a psychopath, Lucas!' she wailed.

'She followed me to your house? When?' he asked more gently, trying to steady his racing pulse and not frighten Poppy any further. He had planned their escape from Teddy so meticulously, but not everything was in place yet. He'd thought they had months left before they would need to leave, as no one would suspect the baby was his... until now! What the hell had happened? Questions were shooting through his mind and Poppy squealed as he squeezed her to him a little too hard. Jemima finding out about them would ruin everything. He knew her well enough to understand that she would never let him leave without a fight. That's why he had planned to get away before she could do anything about it. He was sure she didn't care about him any more, other than as a status symbol, so the fact that she had threatened Poppy made the blood in his veins turn to ice.

'She followed you to my flat about a week ago. She waited for you to go back home, then she came to see me,' she whispered, calmer now that she was back in the safety of Lucas's embrace. 'You'll protect us, Lucas, won't you?'

Lucas led Poppy over to a stool and knelt down at her feet. 'Poppy,' he urged, 'This is really important. What *exactly* did Jemima say?'

Poppy gulped in some air to steady her voice and told him falteringly what had happened. Lucas leaned back on his heels and his mouth fell open. He couldn't believe that Jem would be so brutal. She might hate him now, but to make him think his child was dead and let him bring it up unknowingly made him go to the sink and forcibly vomit the remainder of his breakfast into it. Poppy heaved herself up to comfort Lucas, as she had had a few more days to digest the cruelty of Jem's offer. As she got up she bent double in pain as a strong contraction almost knocked her off her feet.

Lucas wiped his face with a towel and grabbed Poppy before she fell over. Poppy's face was contorted in pain and she started to wail and tried to huddle herself into a ball, covering her stomach. 'I won't let them take my baby, Lucas!' she gasped as another contraction jarred her spine and ran around her stomach.

CHAPTER 33

David walked purposefully into the reception of MAZE's head office and almost took a step back in awe at the opulence of the place. The walls were towers of glass and steel and the main desk swept up from one corner and seemed to swoosh along the whole back wall like a glorious wave of water. It was truly astounding and he felt like he had been swept out to sea before being rescued; a bit shaken up, but alive, and deposited here. The clever lighting of the front desk made the glass give the appearance that flowing water was trapped inside. David felt sure that there must be a water tank feeding it to make it seem so real.

His eyes focused only on the desk and he felt compelled to walk towards it. *What an amazing ploy to draw you in and make you want to stay forever,* he thought. No wonder MAZE were so successful at the building projects they developed, if they all had a creative pull like this one. He wasn't even totally sure why he had decided to call in here. It might be because of an emotional phone call he had received a few weeks before, but was probably because, for all of the buildings the company had developed in different countries, the head office was actually not far from the centre of the nearest town to EVE.

A brightly smiling girl greeted him as he approached the desk and he snapped himself back to concentration. He had done some research on Lucas Trent and wanted to meet the man behind the creation of the sports centre. His secretary, Poppy, had been very forthcoming on the phone, but he hadn't been able to get an appointment to see Lucas. He was just too busy.

David gave the girl at the desk a winning smile and saw the blush creep up her cheeks. He didn't know why he had this effect on women, but just for today, he was going to use it to his advantage. He had dressed carefully, in trousers and a smart shirt. Not enough to be dressy, but not casual enough to arouse suspicion. 'I'm here to meet up with my girl, Poppy,' he beamed at the receptionist, making her grow flustered and knock some papers off her desk.

David smiled kindly at her and she blushed madly and bent to scoop up the papers on the floor. 'Sorry!' she apologised, visibly trying to regain her composure. 'Poppy?'

'She's Lucas Trent's secretary,' he said simply, giving her a friendly wink for good measure.

The girl's eyes widened in shock. 'Poppy?' He heard the next woman along whisper to her colleague, 'That quiet girl on the executive level that's up the duff? This must be the guy who works away and got her pregnant!' she hissed excitedly.

The woman was speaking in hushed tones, pretending to lean down to collect some paperwork from a printer, but David heard her colleague's reply clearly enough. 'The office team on her floor call her *Frozen P*, as in *Frozen Pants,* until they changed it when she got pregnant. Someone obviously managed to break the ice! It's been the talk up there for weeks, with everyone guessing who the father is.'

'What would a gorgeous man like him want with a girl like Poppy?' hissed the girl who'd been printing. She ducked under her desk again, then stood up with a flourish and a handful of freshly printed documents that she placed on her desk.

'Ahem,' said David, trying to recapture the original girl's attention. He'd been taking a long shot on the fact that executive secretaries don't have a lot of free time and are too professional to have boyfriends calling at the office, but now it seemed that Poppy had a boyfriend who was based elsewhere, which suited his story just fine.

The receptionist flushed again and quickly tapped some numbers into the computer screen in front of her whilst picking up the phone. She listened for a moment then frowned. 'I'm so sorry, but Poppy doesn't seem to be at her desk at the moment, which is most unusual. She must be up there somewhere.' She looked flustered suddenly at how unprofessional this must sound to a guest. 'I apologise. I've only been working at MAZE for a few months, and I'm not quite sure of what to do now.'

David smiled at her kindly and leant in, as if to share a confidence. 'I don't often come here, but I would like to see her today. Could I pop up to Mr Trent's office and surprise her?'

The receptionist furtively glanced around them to see who was watching and David saw that her colleagues were all preoccupied with other people now, so she straightened her shoulders as if she was trying to summon some courage, gave David a quick wink, which surprised the hell out of him, and quickly swiped a lift pass to the executive level for him.

'Don't surprise her too much,' she smiled at him, regaining her composure now, 'or you might just bring on her labour!'

David quickly hid the fact that he hadn't had a clue that Poppy was pregnant before today, and swiftly moved towards the executive lift, giving the girl a wave as the doors shut. Phew! He took a huge lungful of air and put his hands on his knees for support. The lift flew soundlessly to the top of the building and before he had time to decide if this was a good idea or not, the doors were gliding open and he stepped out on to the plush carpet of the executive level of MAZE. If Tilly knew what he was up to, she would literally kill him. He should be focusing on the imminent arrival of their own child, but it was because of this that he wanted to make sure the future wasn't about to crumble around them. He knew that it would soon be time for the world to discover what was happening, but he thought that should keep happening gradually, with people finding out the way he had. He didn't want a conglomerate like MAZE to sweep in and decide their futures for them. If someone discovered how to control what was happening, then God help them all!

David started towards the reception desk, which was in front of a glass wall of an office and not towards the open office space. He frowned. There was none of the hustle and bustle of an office environment, and there was no one to be seen at all. He had thought he would have to sweet-talk a few more people, but the place was eerily quiet. He leant over the front of the reception desk to see if there was any paperwork or notices that would give any clues as to where everyone had gone, when he heard a piercing scream and he instinctively dropped the papers he had found and ran into the office. Lucas Trent was standing by the door of the washroom situated at the back of the office and crouching over a moaning girl whom David assumed, by her pregnant state, to be Poppy. David felt his hands curl into fists and he tried to calm his breathing and decide what to do. He grabbed a shocked Lucas and pulled him away from Poppy, sending him flying into a chair by the desk in the main office with an almighty crash, as the chair flew sideways and bounded into the wall.

Poppy gasped at David in horror and he immediately saw his mistake. David moved before Lucas could recover and he picked Poppy up as if she weighed little more than air and sat her on a chair next to Lucas. Another contraction tore across Poppy's stomach and she groaned in pain once again and bent double to try and protect herself from what was happening.

'What the hell?' yelled Lucas, scrambling to his feet and pushing past David to get to Poppy. 'Who are you?' he spat at David. 'And how the hell did you get up here?'

David's brain whirred with all of the possible scenarios he had thought of in coming here, but he had not once imagined he would find Poppy pregnant, and certainly not in labour. Flooring Lucas, the very man he had gone there to try and have a reasonable discussion with, hadn't been his best idea either. Lucas was now staring at him with pure venom in his eyes.

David glanced at the way Poppy and Lucas's hands were entwined, and a warning bell rang inside his head. He quickly recalculated what was going on and thought carefully before he spoke.

'It seems to me that we have a bit of a situation here. Poppy needs medical attention,' he challenged, not answering Lucas's question, but raising one of his own.

Lucas's face flushed in anger. 'How dare you barge in and push me around my own office? Who the hell are you?'

Poppy had tears streaming down her face, but she quietly listened to what David had to say as he crouched down next to her. She looked imploringly at Lucas and David was taken aback at how she seemed to be taking on board whatever was being said.

Lucas stood with his back ramrod straight and gawped at Poppy. She seemed calmer now and was holding on to David with her free hand.

'Lucas, this is David,' she said through gritted teeth as another, not quite as powerful, contraction wound its way from her back to the top of her legs. 'He's come to help us.'

Dr Cole could picture Mr Venner walking around the book-lined walls of his office at home. Dr Cole's mind raced at the possibility of finally discovering the secret that was changing the world. He knew Mr Venner would be lauded as the man who'd saved the planet from extinction, the saviour of mankind, even though he had no scientific expertise of his own. Dr Cole felt bile rise in his throat at the thought.

He had finally had a breakthrough and had told Teddy that he would have the results as soon as both Tilly and Poppy had given birth to their babies.

Dr Cole had been allowed to visit Mr Venner at his home only once, in the early days of their acquaintance. Mr Venner's gardener, Michael, had been busily tending to the trees that lined the impressive driveway, as his boss hated any stray branches to be sticking out, looking at odds with the order he had created in his life. He liked things to be straight up and where he could see them. He didn't hide his wealth or collections from the world. They were on display for all to view. No one would be stupid enough to try and take something that belonged to Teddy Venner, so why shouldn't he have the things he had bought where he could look at them, and admire the skill of the artisans? Dr Cole remembered thinking then that the man was quite mad. How right he had been.

Not many of his peers could afford to buy the trinkets Teddy placed around his house, and some went bug-eyed with envy when they saw how he simply displayed them without a thought about security.

Dr Cole shivered when he saw the screen light up on his phone. He had set it to silent so that he would not be disturbed at this stage of his research, but when Mr Venner called, you answered. He took a huge breath to calm his racing pulse and slowly picked up the receiver.

'Cole?' queried Teddy, although he knew full well that no one else had this number. He knew that saying the man's name made it crystal clear that the doctor was the one under threat if Mr Venner's wishes were not carried out. There was no mistaking his tone of voice or the way he said the name with menace, either. Dr Cole knew that Teddy wasn't asking if it was him who had answered the call. He was asking if the research was complete.

'Almost,' was all Dr Cole could get out of his dry mouth. He cleared his throat and quickly took a sip of water from the glass on his desk. He looked around his gloomy office and wished that he had his team around him. This research was so secret now that one by one they had been shut out of this section of the building. He would need help with the actual births, but afterwards the women would come here, to this unwelcoming, dark room, and they would be scared.

Dr Cole would have to tell them that something had gone wrong, and that they would need to stay there while he tried to save their babies. If he was lucky, he would be able to extract the blood and then reunite the mothers and children. Dr Cole knew that if Teddy had his way, Poppy would never see the light of day again, and his stomach turned over at the thought of what he might be asked to do. He was not a murderer! Didn't Teddy usually have men to do that for him? Dr Cole didn't know if he could follow through on the orders he'd been given, but he also didn't know what alternative he had. Teddy would crush him and his family before he could get his foot out of the door. Dr Cole had stayed away from his own children for years for this very reason, and he felt clammy and sick at the thought of it. He wished he was a stronger man!

He tried to think of a way out of this hole, but there was a brick wall facing him at every turn. Teddy had him cornered and he knew it. That was how he played the game and the reason that he was where he was now. Dr Cole thought of his beautiful daughter. He had tried to see her once or twice, but Teddy had been watching him and had laughed in his face whilst showing him photos of himself cowering behind a wall trying to get a glimpse of her. How she must hate him. She thought he had abandoned her, but he was working towards her future too. Supposing she wasn't able to have children, like many couples now? If he solved this puzzle, then perhaps she would welcome him back when he was an important man. Teddy Venner wouldn't be able to hurt him then, as he would be too valuable. Dr Cole wasn't stupid enough to let Venner know how to correlate his results. Only he would be able to do this. In all the time Venner had thought Dr Cole had been scurrying around doing his bidding, Dr Cole had been encrypting and hiding some of his results. Venner was so sure of himself that he would never believe that Dr Cole would dare, but this was his only way to survive. He knew that otherwise, Venner would destroy him as soon as he found the cure.

Venner was so blinkered that Dr Cole had followed his example and hidden many of his secrets in plain sight. The man was so enamoured with himself that he would never think to look at what was in front of his eyes. If Dr Cole died, then so would the population, as no one else could read his real research. He had devised his own language when he was a student. He was a loner then, someone who didn't communicate easily with others, or fit in with the crowd, so he'd found a way to keep himself busy and used it for one of his theses. His professor had mocked him, but he would be the one having the last laugh. He had carried on developing the language and now no one would understand his research but him. The professor who had scorned him had actually thrown his meticulously-written essays into the bin in front of him, while the whole class had sniggered and looked down on him. Well, he would show them all now. They would have to come to him and grovel to be able to conceive. The ones that ridiculed him would be the first to pay. Financially and emotionally, just like he had had to at university.

A glint of steel came into his eyes and he straightened his aching back. 'It will be done,' was all he needed to say.

CHAPTER 35

Teddy felt elation that everything was falling into place. Dr Cole would be bringing in the girl from the warehouse, the only thing left to do was to get hold of the other one and take her there too. Anyone else walking into MAZE head office would create a stir, so Teddy had decided that the quickest way to get Poppy in front of Dr Cole was to go and get her himself. He was sure she was unaware that her sordid little affair was public knowledge, and Teddy intended for it to stay that way.

Walking into MAZE, Teddy felt the adrenaline hit his system at the way his employees gasped in shock at seeing him there. They then tried to control their reactions and smiled politely at him or carried on working diligently as if nothing untoward had occurred, like the boss walking into the building. Teddy had been visiting a bit more lately, but he had offices everywhere and spent much of his time flying between countries to keep on top of things. The reaction from his staff was why they were working for him in the first place, as he only hired the best, most efficient and productive people. Anyone caught slacking was sidelined and dropped from the employee roster, as soon as he found a way to ease them out. It was all legal, of course, as there were so many rules and regulations these days for workers. He much preferred the old days when you could just get rid of someone who wasn't doing the job the way he wanted them to. Usually putting the fear of God into them made them scamper away with their briefcases between their legs, and one look back told them to keep their mouths shut or they would never again see the light of day.

These days Teddy ran a more respectable business, but he still held on to a few tricks he had learnt from the big boys on the way up. There was always a way to make people want to move on. Luckily, with the calibre of staff he had these days, with many poached from competing firms, he didn't have to worry about any of this. They kept their heads down and performed. The statistics for his business showed that it was still growing, even after all this time. With the ground-breaking research he had pioneered with Dr Cole, he would retire on a high and live like a lord in his castle. In fact, they would probably give him a medal for saving the human race and wiping out any further questions about fertility. He hadn't decided yet how much information he would divulge to the world. He was fairly sure Cole would have some sort of plan to save himself, but Teddy had been keeping an eye on him for years now. He had logs on the way he worked, where he travelled to and who he was in contact with. If Cole thought he was going to walk away from this, with all the information he could inadvertently let slip, he was wrong. He was a dead man walking. Teddy just needed to make sure that the information he had was correct. As soon as Cole concluded his research, he had newer, brighter scientists in his pocket, who could take what Cole had discovered and tailor it to Teddy's requirements.

The lift doors slid silently open and Teddy walked towards Lucas's office. An insipid girl he didn't recognise was sitting at Poppy's desk. She smiled and rose from her chair when she saw him and enquired how she could be of assistance.

Teddy smiled convivially and ignored the fact that his pulse had started to race a little. He had arranged for a training programme for the staff on the upper levels today, so that Poppy would be there alone. He had scheduled the training for the same time as Lucas's board meeting, so that he couldn't interfere with Teddy's plan. What he hadn't prepared for was for this girl to be sitting, looking gormlessly at him, from behind Poppy's desk. He frowned, wondering how he could get Poppy away from the office if there had been a mix up, and she had gone into training instead of this girl. He had purposely meddled with the work load to make Lucas busier than ever, with no time to see Poppy, to isolate her.

'Where's Poppy?' he asked, keeping his tone light and enquiring. 'Or Lucas?'

'I just had a message to cover Poppy's desk,' said the girl simply, totally missing any undercurrents of tension, but probably secretly glorying in the fact that the big boss would now know her face and see what a good job she was capable of. Little did she know that he would forget her as soon as he left the office.

When Teddy looked like he might go, she quickly continued. 'I was told that Poppy had gone into labour, sir, so someone qualified enough to oversee the office was needed at short notice to make sure Mr Trent has everything he needs for our latest building project.'

Teddy's head snapped back to look at the girl again and his eyes narrowed. 'Where is Mr Trent?'

'He went to help get Poppy to the hospital, I think,' she said, probably wondering why he'd bothered, which made Teddy even angrier. This was so embarrassing. 'Mind you, she's not been that organised lately. She's been making mistakes and I've had to type up lots of paperwork more than once for her,' the girl said, digging the knife in Poppy's back while she couldn't defend herself. 'Perhaps she had to beg Mr Trent to take her. Her boyfriend was supposed to be working on the oil rigs, but the rumour mill has gone into overdrive today as it seems he finally showed up on the day she went into labour.'

Teddy waited for further explanation. 'Poppy's boyfriend turned up today,' she reiterated. 'The shock of it must have made her go into labour, as I don't think she was due quite yet.' She suddenly looked like she wasn't really comfortable discussing this with her boss. She gave Teddy her most seductive smile, but he wasn't even looking at her and he stormed past her into Lucas's office and slammed the door behind him.

She stood there, wide eyed, and stared at the phone, as if willing it to ring, but once again, the office fell eerily silent. She sighed and picked up a report she had been typing. 'Bloody Poppy!' she hissed. 'It's always the quiet ones that cause the most trouble.'

Teddy kicked the nearest chair and it flew into the desk and landed in a heap next to another chair already on its side. He walked over to them and wondered what the hell was going on here. What was Lucas thinking of, taking Poppy to the hospital himself? It would be obvious to everyone what was happening if he turned up at the maternity unit with her. There was no way they could swing it that he was just a caring boss once the press found out. No one was stupid enough to believe that.

It meant that the staff at the hospital would have to be convinced that he was a good family friend, and that was an almost impossible task. Teddy quickly scanned his memory banks for the documents he had been reading earlier. Poppy had been going to see a local doctor, but hadn't registered at a hospital yet. He tried to think which one she would go to, as he knew Lucas wouldn't take his mistress to the hospital linked to the fertility clinic where his wife was trying to get pregnant. The next closest hospital was a forty-minute drive away. He shook his arm out to study the golden Rolex on his wrist and calculated that they would still be trying to get there through the city's traffic.

Grabbing the phone, he called a team to try and intercept them on the way to the hospital. He didn't need to say why and they would never ask, they just took orders and obeyed them. He paid a king's ransom to keep it like that, too. The team were all friends, but he knew if the price was right that they would kill one another. Teddy liked it that way. *Friends sometimes made the best enemies. They knew each other's weaknesses and a smart person could always make them turn on each other with a little subterfuge,* he thought with a cruel smile.

His plan to slip quietly away with Poppy was shot to pieces now, so he had to decide how best to handle this. If the press saw him or Lucas with a pregnant secretary, all hell would break loose. Jemima would kill Lucas and she would probably blame Teddy somehow too. With a jolt, he remembered that the girl outside had said a boyfriend had shown up. What boyfriend? Had that little tramp Poppy been sleeping with someone else other than Lucas? If she had, then maybe the baby wasn't even Lucas's! The man had been played for a fool. Of course it was Lucas who couldn't have children and not Jemima. This explained a lot. Poppy had probably seen Lucas's desperation for a child, got pregnant by some cheap boyfriend, been dumped and then decided to seduce Lucas and tell him the baby was his. No wonder she had gone into early labour if the boyfriend had suddenly shown up and come face to face with Lucas.

Teddy called Cole and told him the bare minimum of what was happening. Cole said he had Tilly coming in, so at least that part of the plan was happening. The only way out of this now was to get rid of Poppy in some sort of freak car accident but, before that, to grab Lucas and strangle his sorry arse somewhere else. He couldn't leave any link to the two. Lucas was just causing too much trouble now.

This morning everything had seemed so clear and promising, but Lucas had once again made a mess of things. This could slow the whole process down and if they had to find another mother and child to test the bloods against, who would they use?

Teddy once again punched in the numbers and told his team of the change of plan and to take Lucas and Poppy to Dr Cole, but quietly. Teddy needed to decide what to do fast. Poppy and the baby were key to his plans, so for now they would stay alive. Until they had outlived their usefulness.

CHAPTER 36

Stacey walked up to the café at the EVE warehouse and nonchalantly leaned on the counter, making Lexi start in surprise. 'Stacey,' said Lexi, smiling tightly and running a quick hand through her hair to make it extra bouncy. 'What can I get you?'

Stacey eyed Lexi up and down with a look of apparent distaste at the sight of Lexi in her bright leggings and with her unwavering smile. 'You, little girl, are just begging for a slap around the face,' she hissed under her breath, making Lexi jump. Stacey's delicate little hands bunched into fists and a grimace appeared on her lips. 'Oh, I don't want anything from you, Lexi,' she purred menacingly, with a look of complete distain, 'but it seems that you want something from me.'

Lexi was taken aback by Stacey's frosty glare and the way she was leaning forward so that no one else could hear what she had to say. Lexi stumbled backwards and banged her foot into the side of the cabinet behind her, yelping as the pain shot up her leg. Stacey stared at her in obvious satisfaction, but didn't move away. 'What's your problem, Stacey?' asked Lexi, bending down to rub her aching foot and trying to hide the blush that was mounting at the realisation that Stacey had some sort of issue with her.

'My problem,' said Stacey, smiling sweetly at the top of Lexi's head, 'is the fact that you so obviously fancy my boyfriend and seem to think he is going to drop me and fall at your feet. I can tell you now that it's never going to happen,' she ground out through gritted teeth. 'People have started to talk about you, Lexi.' Stacey cleared a space and hopped her pert little jeans-clad bottom on to the counter so that Lexi couldn't move any further away without causing people to stare.

Stacey made a play of admiring a bracelet that Alfie had given her which was adorning her arm, holding it up to catch the light. Lexi knew she was just rubbing her nose in the fact that no man had ever bought her a trinket like that. 'Even Tilly and David think you are making a show of yourself,' Stacey said. Lexi gasped as the untrue comment hit its mark, so Stacy continued. 'They told me how you tricked Alfie into taking you round to their house. We all see how you moon over him. It's embarrassing, Lexi.'

Lexi stood up, back straight, and stared Stacey right in the eye so that she wouldn't see that she was currently gouging her hand out with her nails, to stop the tears from falling. 'You are mistaken, Stacey,' she said as calmly as she could. 'Alfie and I are good friends. Everyone knows that he's your man.' It felt like acid in the back of Lexi's throat to have to say this out loud. She felt her dreams shatter into a million pieces at Tilly and David's betrayal. She could see them all sitting and laughing at her behind her back. Okay, so she had had a crush on Alfie – but he should never have let her believe she was in with a chance.

She knew really that there was no hope for them, but then Alfie would smile at her and offer to give her a hand with something inconsequential, and she would fall for him all over again. It was his fault that she was in this mess.

Stacey was still sitting admiring her nail polish, as if she hadn't dealt the fatal blow to Lexi's hopes and dreams. She picked up one of the delicately decorated cupcakes that Lexi had just finished icing and threw it straight into the bin behind the counter. Lexi reared forward to grab Stacey, but she was too quick and before Lexi knew it, Stacey had darted away to join a group of men and women sitting by one of the windows enjoying a song-writing session, and Lexi had no choice but to let it go for now.

She looked despondently down at the little crushed cake and slammed some more drinks into the cool cabinet at the end of the serving area. She risked one more glance at Stacey, but she had done what she came to do and was gone. Lexi felt fury rise inside her at how unfairly she had been treated by them all. She had kept away from Alfie as much as she could, but her heart kept pulling her towards him. He had probably been stringing her along all this time, laughing with David and Tilly about her. *That* was what hurt the most. Her supposed friends had turned their backs on her, closing ranks; well, she would show them how disloyal she could be when pushed into a corner. Then they could find out what it was like to be betrayed by someone close to them. The fallout would be the price they had to pay.

Scrubbing back tears from her eyes, Lexi walked over to ask one or two people if David or Tilly were around. She knew they were out, but it helped for others to see her asking. She said she would just check the calendar in David's office to see what appointments they had and scurried to the office before anyone could question her. She opened the door and immediately found what she was looking for.

CHAPTER 37

David's brow was dripping with sweat; he really didn't know how he had got himself into this mess. He grabbed the corner of his t-shirt and dabbed at the front of his face. What had he been thinking of? He had bent down and whispered to Poppy that she was probably in danger and that, if Lucas was the father of her baby, then he was under threat too. Then he'd quickly told her that they needed to get her out of MAZE, with as little fuss as possible.

Poppy hadn't blinked at his suggestion, which had astounded him, and she had even told Lucas that David was there to help them, and to trust him! David was thankful that people listened to him. Tilly always said it was a gift he had been given. Poppy had looked deeply into his startling blue eyes, which had strangely reminded her of someone, and had trusted him completely. She had called out for her mum at that moment and she had to squeeze her eyes shut to stop the tears which were falling down her face. David didn't know where her mum was, but for now she would have to make do with him.

He had managed to get them into his car. They had

calmly walked past the reception desk, after Lucas had told the astounded staff to get cover for his office as Poppy had gone into labour. There wasn't time to get an ambulance, so they were taking her there themselves. Lucas didn't seem to care at this point if they gossiped about him. It was too late to do anything about it now.

It was lucky that David had turned up when he had. With him there, it appeared to the staff that perhaps this was the father of Poppy's baby. If Lucas had had to get her out alone, tongues might have wagged and Teddy could have found out before they even got to the hospital. Once Teddy did find out, they were all dead anyway. David could see that Lucas was in a desperate situation. 'Teddy has kept me so busy lately that I haven't managed to set my own plan in motion, and now we're going to the hospital with a stranger. I don't think this is a good idea,' said Lucas, frowning and looking around as if this would help him come up with a solution to this mess.

David decided it was now or never to find out what on earth was going on. He cleared his throat and quickly made sure that the road in front of him was clear. 'My name's David Love and your company has been working with my students to get them to help with research into your new sports development in Lainstown,' he said slowly in a steady manner, even though he certainly didn't feel calm. David noted the look of confusion on Lucas's face and risked a quick glance at Poppy, who was quietly moaning, but didn't seem to be in so much pain at the moment.

'I came to see you today because something strange is going on and I wanted to find out from you what it is. I can tell already that you don't know what I'm talking about, though, do you?' he sighed, swiping his forehead with the back of his hand and trying to see clearly through the fog of confusion surrounding them.

Lucas rubbed his hand over Poppy's to keep her warm and attempted to make sense of what was happening. 'You are not a friend of Poppy's? Then what the hell are we doing here with you?' he hissed quietly, so that Poppy couldn't hear him. He looked so crumpled and worried in his suit and tie that David could almost feel sorry for the man and the mess he had obviously got himself into.

'I'm guessing the baby is yours?' David said quietly, keeping his eyes firmly fixed on the road. Lucas just sighed and wearily rubbed the back of his neck to ease the cramp that appeared to be setting in. He moved slightly to make Poppy more comfortable. They were in David's van and Poppy was lying across two seats with her head resting on Lucas's legs. Lucas looked really uncomfortable, but Poppy seemed to be dozing now and the contractions had eased off. He didn't dare move her in case they started up again. He was basically trapped in a van, with a total stranger, who could be a raving lunatic for all he knew. David did sympathise, but this wasn't the time for him to be feeling sorry for himself.

'Of course it's mine,' said Lucas through gritted teeth. 'Why else would I be sitting in a van with a complete stranger while my secretary is about to give birth? Where are we going? Poppy is registered with the hospital near where she lives. It's not this way.' Lucas tried to crane his neck to see if he could fathom where they were.

'I'm sorry that I barged into your office and basically manhandled you out of the way,' David said, ignoring the question for a moment while he rallied his thoughts. 'It's the boxer in me.' David smiled to himself. Everyone always assumed that boxers were just sitting around waiting to punch people, although to be fair to Lucas, that was almost what David had done to him. 'I have a weakness for women in need,' he continued, hoping that it might strike a chord with the man sitting behind him in the van. 'It comes from seeing my little sister slapped around the face and thrown down a flight of stairs when we were younger. The stair-wells in our flats had no carpet on them, either. She didn't find it easy to cover up the bruises, but I think by then my stepmother was past caring what people thought anyway. She was usually drunk or off her head on something or other.'

David hoped Lucas was listening to what he was telling him. Lucas probably couldn't relate to seeing a woman struck, but surely he could understand, as a man, how you would want to protect someone... any woman. David turning up as he had was a mad coincidence, but at least Lucas hadn't had to try and get Poppy out alone.

'What did you mean when you said that MAZE was doing research on your students?'

'Didn't know about that, huh?'

'We often carry out targeted research on local areas for a new sports development,' stated Lucas. 'So it's probably that. It's standard procedure. We didn't need to use any for this area, though, as we did another huge sporting village just a few miles away. The research would correlate between both sites as they have such a similar demographic. The Lainstown development is in a very rundown suburb, but those folks aren't our target area, so we wouldn't use them for research, we would ask the other side of town what they were looking for. Plus, I'm running the site. Although I do it from my office, I have been to see the site and it is going to plan.'

'Then why have Dr Cole and his team been crawling all

over the warehouse centre I run for the last few months, questioning all the kids, especially the girls who are pregnant?'

'Dr Cole? Pregnant ones?' asked Lucas with a puzzled look, as Poppy moaned again and clutched her swollen stomach. She was groaning and trying to pull at Lucas now, and he was distracted by the pain on Poppy's sweet face.

'Look,' said David quickly. 'Does Teddy Venner know that you and Poppy are having a baby?'

He looked Lucas straight in the eye for a second before swinging the van into the driveway of a little bungalow, and then driving it straight into a pristine garage and turning off the engine. The look on Lucas's face at the question told David all he needed to know.

'You won't be safe at the hospital,' he said simply.

CHAPTER 38

Dr Cole was still pacing his office when a red light started flashing on his phone. He grabbed it distractedly, happy to have something to do. All of this waiting around for the baby, or babies, to arrive was slowly driving him insane. On the one hand, he would be glad when all this was over, and he would finally have the answers to the questions which had been plaguing him for years, but on the other, he would have to make some hard choices about Tilly and Poppy. There was no real reason for anyone to get hurt with this research, or even realise that they had been part of it, but knowing Teddy Venner, there would be no loose ends left lying around waiting to trip him up later.

He listened to the timid little woman who worked on the outer reception and cursed into the phone. The little messy teenager from the EVE warehouse had turned up and was demanding to see him. Now was not a good time. What on earth could that little brat want with him? She wasn't pregnant, so he had barely spoken to her before, but he had seen those dark eyes watching him. She was a smart kid, that one. It was another reason that he had given her a wide berth. She looked like trouble.

He was just about to bark down the line about not being disturbed, when a thought struck him. He told the receptionist to lead Lexi into the waiting area in front of his office in the main clinic. He wasn't permitted to bring anyone to the section of the building he was sitting in right now.

When he looked out of the little window in the office door, he saw Lexi perched on the edge of a chair and scratching at her bright blue nail polish. Then she started to chew her nails. He wondered if she was having second thoughts about coming here. This had probably seemed like such a good idea at the time, a way to make David, Stacey and the others suffer for the fact that they treated her like a skivvy, but now he could see that she was starting to wonder if she had made a huge mistake, from the way her eyes kept darting around and taking everything in. The place was imposing. He had seen Lexi there once before with Tilly, who said that she had bumped into Lexi on her way out of EVE when Tilly was looking dreadfully pale. When Tilly had explained she was meeting Dr Cole for a check-up, Lexi had offered to go along with her and wait for Tilly in the car. Lexi had probably found the card with the address on in David's office when she was in there. Dr Cole had pinned it in a prominent place last time he'd visited, hoping that one of the teenagers would have a gripe with the others and contact him directly to share their secrets.

Lexi looked like she was feeling pretty intimidated. He didn't want to make her wait too long, but he needed her to be just nervous enough to realise there was no going back now she was there. Everything shone with glass and chrome and was the epitome of cleanliness and professionalism. It looked like no one ever touched anything or walked on the slate floor, as it was so cold and pristine. From the outside, the building looked warm and welcoming. It drew you in from the moment you walked past the reception doors. This part of the building was another matter entirely. Lexi sat on her hands and then started biting her lip. There was the odd person wandering about, but the smooth hushed tones of the place almost gave it a reverent atmosphere, where you didn't dare fracture the silence for fear of breaking the spell it had over you.

A man and a woman sat nervously whispering to each other further down the corridor, but they jumped up and smiled warmly when they were greeted by a doctor in a white coat. The man pumped furiously on the doctor's hand until it was gently withdrawn. The medic led them into the nearest room, shutting the door soundlessly behind him. On the walls were pictures of happy couples holding newborn babies, light and joy shining in their eyes. It was at odds with the vast, empty corridors. There were several rooms along this section of the building and they all looked pretty much the same. There was no individuality here. Lexi wriggled in her chair as if trying find a comfortable position.

She almost jumped out of her seat when Dr Cole came up beside her and placed a cold hand on her shoulder. He was smiling down at her, but the smile didn't quite reach his eyes. She gulped in a lungful of air and grabbed the edge of the chair as if repulsed by his touch. 'Lexi,' he welcomed, as if they were old friends, ignoring the look on her face, remembering a time when he didn't scare teenagers. 'How wonderful to see you. Please come into my office.'

'Oh... I... I think I may have made a mistake,' Lexi gabbled, blushing furiously and looking at the floor. Dr Cole stopped in his tracks.

'Nonsense,' he commanded, sweeping an arm behind Lexi and scooping her into his office; his small, beautifully decorated, but still somehow unwelcoming office. 'Can I get you a drink or anything, Lexi?' he asked solicitously. His eyes narrowed and he quickly calculated how nervous she was and ran through other ways to keep her there.

'No, thank you,' she blustered, and he bet that she was kicking herself for letting him know he was scaring her. She straightened her shoulders and he fleetingly noted how stupid she was to get herself into this predicament. 'I just came to see if Tilly was here. I drove her to her last appointment. She is not at EVE, so I thought she might need a lift home.'

Dr Cole knew she was lying. Her hands were trembling. She was trying desperately hard not to let him know she wanted to get out of the place – and she certainly didn't look old enough to drive. It piqued his curiosity as to why she had really come. His heart soared with the hope that she might finally be there to tell him what was going on at the EVE warehouse. Maybe he wouldn't need to go near Tilly and Poppy at all. He should have just concentrated on the weak ones from the warehouse group, and managed to get some in-fighting going between them. Why hadn't he thought of that earlier, before it was too late? Tilly was due here soon and, from the sound of Teddy Venner on the phone earlier, so was Poppy.

If this little brat was going to spill the beans, then he needed her to do it now. The group had seemed so tight that he had been sure they would never betray each other. Maybe he had been wrong? They had tried to get someone to turn against the others by overpaying the labourers, but they had just gone home and pocketed the money without a word. It had been so frustrating. He was hoping that at least one of them would have let slip that they were getting paid more than everyone else. He had wanted to create jealousy and bitterness, but they all seemed so bloody jolly and happy just to have a job. Perhaps they didn't even know some amongst them were being overpaid? *They must be so thick,* he snarled to himself, before quickly rearranging his face at seeing the odd look Lexi was giving him. Dr Cole once again plastered on a smile and attempted to put an end to this ridiculous charade.

'Tilly's not coming here today, Lexi. She did say that she was really worried about all the things she has to keep quiet about for EVE and you guys. The stress of it all has been making her bleed. She doesn't know what to do and she has been confiding in me, in the hope that I can help her,' he said with care, quickly thinking of the dynamics of the people at EVE. 'Stacey came here too and said she wasn't too keen on you helping Tilly, so I didn't think we would see you here.'

He saw his remark hit home, and felt a small victory at the discomfort of the scruffy girl. She had started picking at her nail polish again and it was leaving chippings all over the pristine floor. He swallowed back his annoyance and continued. 'I hope you don't mind me sharing a confidence, but Tilly told me she is worried about Stacey causing trouble at EVE. She is getting a bit big for her boots and has started telling Tilly and David how to run things.' Dr Cole rubbed his hands in anticipation of his comments causing maximum damage.

Lexi stood up and started pacing around. If Tilly trusted this guy, then perhaps she should too. Lexi's stomach burned with hatred for Stacey. How dare she say who could, and could not, help Tilly when she needed it? Stacey just wanted David, Tilly and Alfie all to herself. She didn't care about other people at EVE. It was all about Stacey, Stacey, Stacey. Well, Lexi felt that, for once, it was about time it was all about *Lexi*. She would be the one to help Dr Cole. If Tilly had already confided some of it to him, then maybe he already knew what Lexi was there to tell him. Lexi tried to listen to her gut instinct, as it had never failed her before, but she was too caught up in the emotion of being betrayed by her friends. She wanted each and every one of them to pay for it.

CHAPTER 39

Poppy groaned from the back seat of the little van, so David jumped out to open the door for Lucas. Lucas felt like his legs had gone to sleep with the weight of Poppy leaning on them, and he had to drag himself out of the seat and shake some life into them. He helped get Poppy into a sitting position and eased her swollen stomach past the door whilst lifting her gently into his arms. He looked around frantically to try and make some sense of what had happened in the last hour of his life.

David had disappeared inside the little bungalow and then reappeared with an old woman in a very bright, wrap-around dress. 'This is Lucille,' explained David, as if that would solve the problems of the world. Poppy gave a scream of pain and Lucas hurriedly followed the pair of them inside, as they placed her gently on the bed in the centre of a pretty little room to the immediate right of the front door.

'What the hell is going on?' raged Lucas, staring anxiously down at Poppy. He felt like he was being swept along on a tidal wave and his life was now out of his control. 'If we don't get her to a hospital, she could lose the baby!'

'She will be fine, young man,' smiled Lucille, patting him on the arm reassuringly. 'She's in the final stages of labour and you wouldn't be able to move her now, even if you wanted to. Of course, call an ambulance by all means, but they will arrive after your baby is born.'

Lucas frowned at the woman's calm manner and the fact that she didn't even blink at all of these strange people turning up out of the blue at her immaculate little home. She bent down to smooth Poppy's brow before turning to talk to David and issuing a string of orders about what he needed to do. He dashed out of the room and returned moments later with a medical bag and a huge pile of fluffy towels in an array of moss tones. Lucas felt like he had dropped off the side of the Earth and been stuffed into a parallel universe. He was too shocked to move and his mind was flying everywhere in a panic about how to grab back the reins and regain control of the situation. He could command boardrooms full of people, but today, right here, he felt completely lost.

'Lucas,' said David, kindly trying to distract him from the distress Poppy was in. 'This is Lucille. She works with me. She's a trained midwife. Poppy is in safe hands.'

Lucas let out the breath he hadn't known he was holding and looked forlornly down at Poppy's hunched form. She was quieter now and seemed to be listening to what the older woman had to say. 'Surely we need to get Poppy to a hospital? She can't give birth here!' he said angrily, pacing up and down the small room. Poppy gave him a pleading look as if they had finally found a way out of this mess and she wasn't about to let her guardian angels go without a fight.

'Please, Lucas,' she gasped as another almighty contraction hit her and she wailed in agony. Lucas grasped her hand, ready to do whatever she asked to take the pain away. 'I've been so scared and I've had no one to turn to,' she managed once she had caught her breath again. 'Jem threatened to kill all of us or take my baby. You kept telling me to wait until you'd found a way out, well, it's too late for that, Lucas! David came here to get some answers from us. He didn't need to get involved in all this, but he's helped us anyway,' she said, showing that she had been aware of their hushed conversation in the car. 'Mr Venner would never let us bring up our child together and neither would Jem. We both know that hiding is the only option left to us.'

'But, Poppy,' stammered Lucas, feeling out of his depth for the first time in his life. 'I was making plans to get us away from here. I told you about them.'

'The plans weren't ready in time, Lucas,' said Poppy fiercely, shocking Lucas to the core as she wrapped her hands protectively around her heaving stomach. 'We are about to be parents, and I am not waiting around like a sitting duck to be picked off by the Venner family.'

David stood back admiringly but listened carefully to the discussion between Poppy and Lucas. Then Poppy's face contorted in pain once more. He quietly let himself out of the room, and grabbed his phone to call Tilly and fill her in on the latest drama surrounding them all.

Moments later, David slammed the phone back down on Lucille's coffee table and cursed Tilly for not having her phone with her. He picked it up again and dialled EVE in the hope that she would be there.

Tilly's phone began to buzz gently in its hiding place, under a pile of papers on David's desk. A few stray sheets fell off the top of the pile at the vibration and floated gently to the floor, but otherwise the room stayed silent.

Alfie opened the office door and peered around with a quizzical look on his face. 'Stacey!' he yelled at the top of his voice, which made her look up and smile at him from where she was perched on the side of a table chatting to a group of girls.

She jumped up and sashayed over to him, giving him a come hither stare. He shook his head to clear the image of her lithe legs clad in skin tight jeans and tried to remember why he had called her. She laughed and gave him a quick kiss on the nose before looking behind him into the office. 'No Tilly?' she asked. 'Although I've noticed that Lexi's absent too, and I'm glad that for once I don't have to witness her incessant drooling over you, Alfie.'

'I thought I heard a phone,' Alfie remembered, ignoring her sniping. 'Did you leave yours in here?' Stacey walked over to the desk and picked up the sheets of paper lying on the floor. As she was putting them back in the pile she noticed Tilly's pink phone case. Grabbing it, she turned a worried face to Alfie.

'This is Tilly's phone! She never goes anywhere without it. David would literally kill her, especially now that the baby is due. Have you seen her?' she asked quickly, pushing past him and scanning the people at EVE to see if her friend was snuggled into a corner somewhere.

Alfie came up behind Stacey and took the phone in his hand. 'I haven't seen David either. Do you think the baby's come?' he asked with concern. Stacey clicked open the phone and typed in Tilly's password. 'Stacey!' yelped Alfie. 'You can't do that! And how do you know Tilly's password?' he demanded to know.

'Oh, I know everyone's password,' she quipped. 'I just pay attention at the right times,' she winked at him. Alfie shifted uncomfortably from foot to foot and put his hand in his pocket to make sure his phone was still there. 'You don't need to worry,' she smiled. 'There's nothing on your phone that troubles me!'

'Stacey!' he shouted, almost stamping his foot in rage. 'You cannot do that!'

'I just did,' she said, waiting for the picture to slide from Tilly's phone and then checking recent texts and voice-mails. She listened carefully whilst playfully swatting Alfie's hand away from her backside, then her face fell as she heard David's worried message.

The phone rang again, making Stacy jump, but Alfie grabbed it and answered it on the second ring. David sounded taken aback as Alfie always left it to someone else to answer the phone.

'Is Tilly there?' David quickly asked. 'I don't have time to muck around today, Alfie.'

'She's not here, mate,' said Alfie, trying to hold Stacey away from the phone before giving in with a small yelp. Stacey gave a grunt of satisfaction that the sharp heel of her shoe had hit home on Alfie's foot and she snatched the phone from him.

She didn't bother with pleasantries and told David exactly what else she had heard on Tilly's phone. David threw the phone back onto the table at Lucille's house with a loud crack – and the screen cracked and died.

CHAPTER 41

Dr Cole was sitting behind his desk and staring at the kid in front of him. He could see the indecision on her face and knew now that she had come to blow the whole thing up. He could have danced around the room with glee, but had to tread really carefully. He had Tilly arriving soon and didn't want to miss her, or let the two girls see each other.

'Tilly has been so stressed of late about the secrets she has to keep,' he hedged. He had seen the way this girl mooned over the big fella with the booming voice. His researchers had also told him that they had seen his girl-friend's hackles rise time and time again.

'She told me that she thinks Stacey is trying to take over at the warehouse. Tilly feels that when she has the baby, Stacey will tell everyone else what is happening, and then all hell will break loose.' he calmly sat back to see what reaction his words would get.

Lexi's face flamed at the mention of Stacey and Dr Cole knew that his poisoned arrow had hit its mark. 'Tilly told me that Alfie is getting fed up with Stacey's interfering and asked me if I could help to control the situation. If everyone finds out, it could get messy.'

Lexi's shoulders slumped in confusion, but she didn't look convinced.

'I think Tilly was a bit confused as to why Stacey doesn't want you around either?' he threw in. 'Tilly thought Stacey must have a reason and was going to ask her. She said it might be something to do with Alfie. Whatever that means,' he said casually, whilst watching her from hooded eyes.

Lexi jumped up and swore loudly. 'Stacey knows nothing about me. How dare she say I'm not allowed around Tilly? Does she think I would hurt the baby or something? She's the one who can't stand the sight of kids and thinks they are just annoying bags of noise. She would probably faint at the first sight of a dirty nappy anyway. She's turning them all against me. Just because she doesn't want me around Alfie!'

Dr Cole cast a shrewd glance at Lexi and decided he had bided his time long enough. 'Well, I suppose you can't put all the blame on Stacey, when her boyfriend so obviously likes having girls fighting over him. I've seen him giving you encouragement many times. I've seen the way he looks at you. She is probably just jealous. Tilly did say David had reservations about you too, though.'

Lexi gasped as if she had been hit and stumbled back into her chair. She drew a sharp breath and her eyes narrowed at Dr Cole. She needed to calm her nerves, stop the adrenaline flowing through her veins and slow her heart rate back to normal, before she keeled over on the spot. He needed her to be coherent enough to tell him what he needed to know and his patience was wearing thin.

He grinned to himself as he could see she was so angry

now, she would want to make those idiots at EVE suffer for all the horrible things they had been saying about her behind her back. Especially the ones he'd made up. She stared straight at him, squared her shoulders, and started to talk.

CHAPTER 42

Jem walked into the reception of MAZE and was gratified to see several pairs of eyes look up and then lots of straightening of backs and welcoming smiles directed her way. She ignored all of them and walked up to the executive lift, jabbing her brightly painted talon at the defenceless button and tapping her skyscraper heels restlessly while she waited the thirty seconds for the lift to glide down to her. As soon as the doors opened she was inside and pressing the button for Lucas's floor.

She wished she felt calmer about what she was about to do, but it was time to put her plan into action. Poppy must be even more enormous by now and the girl needed to know her place. Jem pulled on the side of her pencil straight skirt to bring the hem into line and undid one of the top buttons of her blush pink silk blouse. A little cleavage wouldn't harm, to draw Lucas's attention away from the little brown mouse on the reception desk outside his office. It couldn't be that hard. The girl was a complete drudge.

Jem was going to tell Lucas they had found a baby to adopt, then she would make her father move Lucas to a different part of the country, where the little brown mouse couldn't follow. Jem would make sure she didn't follow, or her sorry little arse would pay for it.

Teddy would question why she wanted to relocate for all of ten seconds, then would assume she was bored and do as she said. He might not have time for Jem, but he always did what she wanted when it came to houses, cars and jewellery. She supposed that, as her father had even picked Lucas for her, he'd decided what she would want in a man and went out and found it for her. Perhaps he did love her in his own way. She grimaced at the thought. She wished they had a normal family life, but this was the father she had, so she might as well get the most out of him.

The lift doors opened noiselessly, and Jem was about to place one stilettoed foot on the carpeted floor when her father stormed out of Lucas's office with a face like thunder. She almost faltered in her step. She wasn't ready to face her father yet. He would be able to tell in an instant that she was up to something; he'd always had the ability, even when she was tiny. She could never get away with anything when he was around. That's why she had always heaved a sigh of relief when he was away on business, then demanded his attention the moment he returned home. She felt her face grow hot and then decided she had no choice but to step out of the elevator and face him. He had almost run into her before he became aware she was there, and when he did, his head snapped up in shock. 'Jemima! What brings you here today? I thought you hardly ever visited Lucas at work these days?'

Jem raised an immaculately sculpted eyebrow and took in her father's ruffled expression and less than perfect tie. She reached out to straighten it for him and for a moment he seemed at a loss for what to do. Then he remembered where he was and smiled warmly at his daughter. This made her even more suspicious about what was wrong with him.

'Daddy,' she said with a slight frown. 'Is everything okay? Have you been to see Lucas?'

Jemima glanced at the blonde girl who was sitting where the little brown mouse usually sat and saw she was watching them with interest. This was probably the best thing that had ever happened to her in her dreary life. Not only had she met the legendary Mr Venner, but now she had seen his daughter close up, too. She would probably dine out on that bit of gossip for months. Jemima looked pointedly at the pile of paperwork in front of the woman, who blushed, ducked her head and busied herself with the first sheet.

Teddy shepherded his daughter into Lucas's office and quietly shut the door behind him. 'He had already left when I got here,' stated Teddy, his gaze roaming his daughter's face, as if trying to work out how he could shield her from some terrible news, which made her stomach start to ache. 'Perhaps you'll find him at home?'

Jem frowned and wondered why her father was behaving so strangely. 'Lucas never comes home during a working day, Dad. You know that. Did you have a meeting scheduled?'

Teddy reached out for the cut crystal bottle of brandy on the discreet bar at the back of Lucas's office, and poured hefty slugs into two tumblers. Some of the liquid sloshed over the rim of one of the glasses and he cursed quietly under his breath, seemingly playing for time, and slowly turned to face his daughter.

'You know, don't you?' she said simply, walking over and taking the glass from him before drinking the contents in one swift movement, wincing at the taste. She never once took her eyes from her father to give him time to work out a way to lie to her.

Teddy almost choked on the amber liquid and quickly coughed and released some air from his lungs. 'Bloody Lucas! I'm not going to pretend that I don't know what you're talking about, Jemima,' he said gravely. 'I haven't known long, but I wanted to confront Lucas about it myself before I decided what to say to you.'

'You don't think I had a right to know that my husband is screwing half his office staff?' she screeched, throwing the glass at the table and hearing a satisfying crack as it broke into a thousand tiny shards and dropped to the floor.

'Hardly half of the staff, Jem,' he consoled, but seeing the fire in her eyes he stepped back and kept his distance. He grimaced as he turned at the same time she did, and Jem noted the girl outside was on the phone. Teddy threw his hands up in frustration. 'She'll have heard the crack of the glass and will no doubt be asking downstairs what to do.' He quickly walked to the door and looked at the girl with a soft smile. 'I do apologise, but I just knocked over one of Lucas's sculptures. It has broken a glass on his desk. Don't worry about it, I'll arrange housekeeping on my way out. I under-stand that this would usually be Poppy's job, but it's your first day.' He smiled again and the girl blushed to the roots of her hair, mumbled something into the phone, and rapidly placed it back on the desk.

Closing the door behind him once again, Teddy looked down at his daughter, who was now slumped on the leather couch at the side of the office. Her face was covered with her hands and he asked her if she was crying, not bothering to offer her any comfort, but sounding irritated, like she was being a nuisance again. 'I will kill Lucas for this!' he seethed, but when Jem looked up, he saw that instead of tears, she had hatred in her eyes.

'How dare you know about this and not tell me? I have never been good enough for you,' she screeched at him.

Teddy looked at his daughter and raised an eyebrow in shock at her behaviour, as if she was being unnecessarily wilful. He took a step towards her, and the movement made her quake and quickly remember who she was facing. Her father had never raised a hand to her, but then he had never had to. She had tried every way to push his buttons whilst she was growing up, but she had always known when she had pushed too far, and when it was time to back off and play the little girl lost. Her father was mostly immune to tears, but he didn't like anyone else to upset his children nonetheless. She recalled how she had cried, when she'd told her father her best friend at school had hit her. It wasn't true, but Jem had wanted to see how he would react. Funnily enough, the girl and her family moved away soon after, and Jem had found a new best friend. She had always wondered about that time.

Jem looked mutinously at her father but he just pulled a chair out and sat her down in it. 'Don't be ridiculous, Jemima,' he scolded as if she was still a small child. 'I've only just found out, and if I had told you, what good would it have done? I wanted to sort this mess out before you got involved.'

I'm already involved! Jem seethed, trying to calm herself down and not slap his amazingly annoying face. She knew if she ever did that, then she would be laid flat out on the floor in seconds. She had seen the way her father dealt with disobedience. When she was a teenager, she had once crept up to the door of his office at home and overheard him 'dealing with' one of his staff. The staff member never came back out of the door, while Jem had hidden at the top of the stairs and waited for hours and hours.

She stared up at her father defiantly and felt a smile creep on to her face as her eyes blazed brightly up at him. 'You should have given me enough credit, letting me know what was happening sooner. Poppy is giving me the baby and Lucas will be none the wiser.'

She felt a flicker of adrenaline as she saw her words hit their mark and she stood up to face her father at last. 'I have already been to see that stupid girl and told her how this is going to pan out. I'm going to tell Lucas that I've found a baby to adopt. Poppy will say the baby has died in child-birth and Lucas and I will bring up the child.'

Teddy appeared to look at his daughter with fresh eyes and really see her, for the first time. 'You really are extraordinary. How could I have missed it? You could be a real asset to me, darling.' He started pacing the room, but had a manic grin on his face now. 'I'm not getting any younger, but I had dismissed you as too frivolous. How wrong I have been. It is so rare for me to miss something like this.' He walked over and grabbed her arms a little too roughly for her liking. 'You're just like me, Jem. To make a man bring up his own child without his knowledge is distilled poison. I could use a girl like you. My own plan was to make Lucas and Poppy disappear, but perhaps your way of thinking has some merit.' He looked speculatively at her, more animated in her presence than she had ever seen him.

'You're right, Jemima. I should have trusted that you are a grown woman and fully able to handle this situation as you see fit.'

Jem could have almost fainted at the words coming from her father's mouth. He was regarding her strangely, as if he had never fully known her before. 'I am more than capable of handling my husband, Daddy,' she said. 'If that insipid girl thinks she can waltz in and take him, then she can think again. Once my plan is in action, we won't hear from her again. She knows not to mess with me and she has no one to help her. She is completely isolated here. I've checked. So, where is the little brown mouse?'

David paced back and forth across the room and tried not to think too much about the wails of pain coming from the next room. It had been over an hour now, but there was still no sign of a baby. Lucille had said there was no time for an ambulance, but he could see now that she was just trying to stop Lucas from moving Poppy anywhere else and he was grateful for that. He tried once again to get his mangled phone to limp back to life and cursed himself for the loss of control that made him throw it in anger. It had been such a long time since he had let his emotions overcome him, but his anger at Tilly for leaving her phone behind was all consuming. Where the hell was she?

He looked out of Lucille's window again and ran to the door when he saw Alfie and Stacey pull up on her driveway. David was glad he hadn't stopped Alfie from replacing the old relic he usually drove around in. It had been barely hanging together with a few strategically placed nuts and bolts. It was only because Stacey had flatly refused to be seen dead in it any more that he had finally conceded and given the old girl the push. This new car was an improvement.

David totally ignored his friend and grabbed Tilly's phone from him.

'I'll dismiss your rudeness as I appreciate that now is not the time to discuss manners,' Alfie joked, clearly trying to lighten the atmosphere. Stacey frowned when a screech of pain resonated from the bedroom and David quickly ushered them inside the building.

Alfie shot David a questioning glance but Stacey just stood in the middle of the room with her hands on her hips, her demeanour showing she demanded to know what the hell was happening. 'The phone code, Stacey?' was all David said, as if standing in Lucille's lounge with a poor woman crying in pain next door was an everyday occurrence.

'Is Tilly in there now? Did you find her?' said Stacey, trying to push past him to get to Tilly. 'I don't understand why you aren't in there with her, tough guy. Is Lucille helping her give birth?' Her nose scrunched up as if the idea didn't appeal to her.

Stacey tried to manoeuvre around David to get into the other room, but Alfie held her arm firmly as she passed and she gave a yelp in protest. 'I don't think that's Tilly, Stacey,' he said, still staring at David.

'It's my sister, Poppy,' said David simply. 'She's having a baby, but we didn't have time to get her to the hospital.'

Lucas, who had just walked into the room to get Poppy some water, froze in obvious horror. 'Your sister! Why didn't you both tell me you are related?' he stormed at David.

'She doesn't know. I don't think our mother ever told her,' said David simply.

'Who the hell is that?' asked Stacey, eyeing Lucas

warily. Lucas stared straight back at her and answered for David.

'I'm Lucas... the father of Poppy's baby.'

Stacey screwed up her eyes in concentration and looked on in confusion, but David could imagine her brain whirring, trying to put the pieces of this puzzle together. Stacy was smart and it wouldn't take her long. 'Don't you run the MAZE group? I remember seeing a piece about you and your gorgeous wife in a glossy mag.' David decided not to add that Lucas's wife, Jemima, had all but made Stacey swoon with jealousy at the life she lived. Closets full of clothes, a rich husband, fast cars and an adoring daddy, apparently. He knew that Stacey looked at Alfie and wondered why she stayed with such a hulk of a man, but then she always sighed and said that her heart melted at the sight of him, so he hoped she realised why, before Lexi sidled in and stole him from her.

'Oh...' mumbled Stacey, blushing to the roots of her hair and she quickly pushed past him to see if Lucille needed anything. 'Where is Tilly, then? Was I right about that message on her phone and she's with Dr Cole? You don't think she's gone into labour too, do you?' she called over her shoulder as Lucas followed her back into the room, as if this strange collection of people was suddenly the norm in his afternoon's schedule and he had abandoned fighting his predicament.

'That's the problem,' ground out David. 'I don't know.'

Alfie went and put an arm around his friend's shoulder, and patted his back to show his support. 'Has Tilly called you?'

David signalled to the smashed phone on the floor and Alfie passed David the piece of crumpled paper in his hand on which he had scribbled Tilly's phone code and handed it to David. David immediately tapped the number in and began scrolling through Tilly's texts and listening to her messages.

'Stacey was right,' David said to Alfie, looking really worried now. 'There is a message from Dr Cole and I bet she went there to talk to him in person. I need you to help me find her, Alfie. Poppy seems scared half to death of Edward Venner and Lucas isn't giving me any confidence in him either. It looks like Lucas was planning to hide himself and Poppy away.'

'They're both frightened,' David continued. 'If Cole is working for Venner, then why is he being so cordial to Tilly? By the sound of it, it's something to do with our baby and they were possibly going to try and get Poppy in to the clinic too. It has to be connected with our suspicions about the birth rate. Poppy won't be safe in a hospital.'

David began to pace the room and bunched his fists while he looked around for something or someone to punch to ease his frustration. He hadn't resorted to violence for years, though, and he made his hands relax and stood still for a moment, whilst he formulated a plan. 'We need to keep them hidden for now. Lucille is pretty relaxed about the whole thing and doesn't seem concerned about this birth.' He looked up as Stacey returned to the room looking shaken and dazed.

'I'm never, ever going through that!' she said, almost snarling and looking appalled. 'That woman is going through trauma in there and the man is just pacing and mumbling to himself. He looks like he's in seven stages of hell and someone needs to go in there and give him a smack around the face.'

Alfie went and grabbed Stacey's hand, making her stare questioningly at his agitated manner. He stared at her pleadingly, and she started to back away from him. 'Oh no!' she said firmly. 'I am not staying here to babysit this lot.'

'Please, Stacey,' implored David. 'They are not safe anywhere else. This is all getting out of hand, and it seems that Edward Venner knows that his son-in-law has got Poppy pregnant. He's not happy about it and we can't let him find them. Not yet anyway.'

CHAPTER 44

Alfie grabbed the keys and he and David raced to the car. Without saying a word, Alfie steered towards the clinic. 'What is the situation with Poppy?' Alfie asked gently, testing the subject.

David sighed and rubbed his temples. 'Mum vanished when I was little, as you know, Alfie. She just disappeared off the face of the Earth. I looked for her for months. I used to plead with my dad to tell me where she had gone. He just gave me a smack round the ear and told me to give it up,' David flinched as if he could still feel his father's hands hitting his face. 'In the end he got fed up with my wailing. He told me to take a good look at myself, and said that she ran off without a backward glance in my direction. Why would I think she would worry about a little piece of shit like me?'

Alfie winced. He had heard some things about David's mum, but had never got to the bottom of the story about why she'd left. It was because David himself didn't know, but Alfie had always felt that there was more to the story. His friend was a private person when it came to his mum and Alfie had never pushed him to talk about it. Now he wished he'd been a better friend.

'She contacted me a couple of months ago and told me, right out of the blue, that I had a sister! She hadn't heard from Poppy for a while and was worried. She cried and pleaded for my help.' At Alfie's sharp intake of breath he carried on. 'I thought the only reason she could leave me, was if she was dead. But it seems my dad was right after all. It was like she had floored me with one punch. I had kind of assumed she had to be dead, why else would you leave an eight-year-old child with a masochistic bully like my dad?'

'She must have had her reasons,' countered Alfie, trying wildly not to growl and fill the car with profanity that she didn't deserve such a kind and devoted son. He knew that David's mother had been as timid as a mouse. He'd once heard his own parents saying how she rarely left the house and veritably jumped out of her skin once when his own dad had put a hand out to help her with her heavy shopping bags on one of her rare appearances outside before she disappeared. David had confided in Alfie about the horror of growing up with a father who was determined to squash his spirit and a mother who loved him, but was too scared to even look at him sometimes, in case she earned a punch in the lower back from his dad. It was always somewhere where no-one else would see the deep purple bruises his fists left behind. Alfie's heart went out to the young David and the suffering he had endured as a child... that he still endured today.

Alfie placed a consoling hand on his friend's shoulder, shaking David out of his reverie. The action nudged Alfie into concentrating more on keeping the car on the road, and suppressing, for now, the anger and injustice he felt on behalf of his friend. It seemed to be taking them so long to get to Tilly.

'My mother said she thought my dad was still alive,' said David quietly, glancing at his friend before staring resolutely ahead again.

'He died years ago, though,' said a surprised Alfie.

'I know, but apparently he threatened to kill both of us if she ever tried to contact me, or take me with her.'

Alfie slammed his fist against the dashboard, making David jump and his face crease into a frown. 'She wouldn't believe that, surely?' Alfie asked incredulously. David just shrugged and Alfie looked for the turn-off that would bring them closer to Tilly – and Dr Cole's throat. He knew that David would strangle the man with his bare hands if he had touched even one bouncy red hair on Tilly's head.

'She said her husband doesn't know about me, either,' David continued almost as if he couldn't quite take in what he was saying. 'He's very set in his ways and wouldn't understand why she had lied to him. She said she lived in fear of Dad finding her and of her husband discovering her secret. She worried about Poppy's safety if my dad ever found out about her,' he said. 'She might not even be legally married as she was too scared to ask Dad for a divorce, or tell her new husband why she couldn't marry him. She just let Dad think she was dead, by dropping off the edge of the Earth. She thought it would be safer for me. She wrote me loads of letters but couldn't send them. She gave them to me.' He looked out of the side of his eye to see if Alfie was listening, as he had gone really quiet.

'What did they say?' asked Alfie sadly, trying not to say anything against David's mother that would upset him further. Alfie couldn't understand how a mother could leave her child, but then he had never had to live in terror, like David's mum.

'I don't know. I haven't plucked up the courage to read them yet,' he shrugged. 'She said her husband is really traditional. She's a housewife, she cooks and cleans and he looks after her in return. She was scared that she would lose the only security she has ever had, if she told him the truth about her past. She was frightened of losing his love and respect, but she did sound relieved that she wasn't a bigamist,' he said, laughing a bit manically for Alfie's liking.

'That's not love,' ground out Alfie. 'It's control again!'

'I know,' sighed David, 'but she's not strong like you, Alfie. She had any individuality beaten out of her years ago by Dad. She's been living in fear her whole life. Even after she realised that Dad wasn't looking for her any more.'

Alfie bit down on his bottom lip and tried to control his anger. He didn't want to upset his friend, but he felt a deep sense of loss for the young David who had always idolised his mother and had resolutely believed that she would return for him one day. It seemed now that the only reason she came back was, once again, to protect herself above all others, her only son included.

David nodded towards the latest road sign and Alfie realised that they were almost at the medical facility that Tilly had been going to, to visit Dr Cole. They had already checked it out when they heard underground whispers about what went on there. There was nothing concrete or factual about the information. If there had been, they wouldn't have let the MAZE team near the kids at the warehouse, or Tilly. David had wanted to go there with her for every appointment, but the timings had never seemed to work out. Alfie remembered Lexi saying something to Tilly about being run down when she arrived with the cupcakes and Alfie bet that David was kicking himself for not following it up. EVE took up so much of his time that he could easily be distracted, but Tilly was his priority and he should have found out what Lexi had meant. He wondered now if Tilly had been throwing David a curveball and keeping him away. He frowned and wracked his brain to try and think of any reason why she would do this, but came up blank.

David had told him that MAZE did medical testing, as this was how they made their health supplements. He hadn't heard anything about how the tests were done as the company had created a very careful veneer of respectability, but he still felt that something shifty went on there. They should have kept Tilly away, and not encouraged her to get medical advice from them. If only they had heard the whispers before Tilly had met Dr Cole.

There was no way David would have let Tilly go there without him if he'd thought there was anything suspicious going on, but it now seemed that she had been a regular visitor without his knowledge. Even Lexi seemed to know more than David did. *What had Tilly been playing at?* he fumed.

He rounded the corner of the car park and screeched to a halt in front of the building's entrance. They both scrambled out, not caring if someone shouted at them to move the car.

CHAPTER 45

As the two men ran along the hall, the receptionist glanced up from the serene reception area, alarmed at the sight of such imposing men storming towards her. She rushed out from behind her plush leather desk, feeling as if her heart was going to burst inside her chest. She had never been trained what to do in a situation like this. These guys looked like they meant business with their bulging muscles and jean-clad thighs. Her eyes were glued to David's impressive physique before she realised how close they were getting. She could have kicked herself for gawking, wasting precious moments that let them get further into the building before she'd decided how to react.

Normally, she wouldn't bat an eyelid at anyone coming in, but for some reason these guys were not stopping to wait for someone to escort them from reception and they didn't look like they would listen if she politely requested them to leave. No-one had ever spoken out of turn to her before. The couples that came in were always almost spookily quiet. They hardly spoke, let alone barging through doors and storming into reception, looking mutinous.

She looked at the men in dismay as they waltzed past her without so much as a flicker of recognition, while she stood there like a dumbfounded penguin, arms at her sides, hands flapping ineffectually. *She wasn't trained for this type of situation*, she raged silently, looking at them. Who the hell did they think they were, strutting in here like this and ignoring her existence? They looked like a couple of thugs, albeit gorgeous ones! She gave herself a mental slap for being distracted by their biceps. They were rude and messy and they didn't belong here.

She certainly wasn't about to go and follow them. Supposing they had a knife? She had read in the newspaper just that morning about how crime rates were dropping further, but she wasn't taking any chances with the likes of them. What on earth were they doing there?

She gathered her wits and scurried quickly to the security office which was located on the other side of the building. Tony, their burly security guard, was supposed to be prowling the corridors, but he was usually pretty lax about it as there were high tech security cameras everywhere. *Though what good were they when he never even looked at them?* she fumed silently.

Tony's job was so boring, as no one raised their voice above a whisper, that he spent most of his days in the nurses' canteen, chatting up the prettiest of them, making them giggle and flirt. He always said that he loved his job. She could see why, as he got paid to sit and chat with the nurses and his bosses rarely checked up on his commitment to his job. He had to file a daily report, but he had taken to writing seven at once, then sending one each night, the lazy pig. They were always almost identical, too, as she had to file them on her computer each morning. He only ever had to change the occasional word or two. He just had to show his face to the security cameras every once in a while and he was sound, he often bragged, making her fume as her job was to look immaculate and always be on call. She had to smile at clients all day even if she had her period or she'd had an argument with her boyfriend, not that she had a boyfriend, as she was always at work.

She could see that the big black man almost had to run to keep up with the blonde muscly one, as he randomly shoved open doors as they went. She knew that the rooms were all deserted, apart from one, which had a tense couple inside who looked up hopefully when she opened the door to see if the men were in there, but they had disappeared. She quickly apologised for disturbing the couple and backed out of the room, leaving them in a little huddle on their chairs once more.

She glanced around, her pulse racing, and spotted them further along the building. Making a decision, she turned around and began racing back to give Tony a swift kick and to yell at him to get off his big behind and start actually earning his wages.

As David and Alfie neared the end of the corridor, there was one last door, which was set apart from the rest. It had its own little waiting area with several chairs tucked along one wall and a simple reception desk in the same colour as the walls, so it seemed to flow seamlessly from the floor. The chair behind the desk was empty, but a tall girl with waves of nut-brown hair looked startled at the sight of the two men as she walked through the adjacent door to a small kitchen area. She held a tray of iced Coca-Cola and a plate of delicious-looking biscuits. She smiled questioningly at them, then her smile faltered as they ignored her and grabbed the handle of the door to the last office.

She quickened her pace, which wasn't easy considering

the tray she was balancing in one hand, and she tried to get rid of it whilst still looking professional and attentive. She grabbed the phone on the desk which was connected to reception and buzzed through. 'There are two new clients here who haven't checked in at this desk, and I don't know if I should barge in and ask them what they are doing here?'

'I don't recall any more appointments today, I'm not even entirely sure why Dr Cole has an office here at all,' she added. 'I spend most of my days fielding calls for him and then passing them on to another office.' The reception staff always secretly wondered if Dr Cole was some sort of secret agent, as he often looked furtive and harassed, glancing over his shoulder whenever he came in and jumping at the merest sound.

The girl slammed the phone down and stood up, finally managing to balance the tray before the Cola slipped and smashed on the immaculate floor. She looked after David and Alfie as they entered Dr Cole's office and disappeared inside, leaving the door open behind them. She pressed a buzzer under her desk and cursed the security team for being so lackadaisical. 'Where are you?' she fumed.

Alfie looked over his shoulder through the open door of the last office and saw a security guard approaching, with the first receptionist peeking out from behind his considerable bulk. She had a worried look on her face as she approached the woman they had just brushed past. Alfie urgently hurried David through the inner door to the left. 'If we don't get a move on, we might be thrown out before we find Tilly.'

Lexi jumped up in alarm from where she had been huddled on the couch at the back of the room. She looked up at Alfie when she saw him standing behind David, and a feeling of pure relief wound its way through her.

'Lexi!' hissed David. 'What the hell are you doing here? Did you come with Tilly?' he glanced round the room looking like he was trying desperately to quell the panic that was gnawing at his insides. She had never seen him upset before and her lip wobbled. Now was not the time to lose it. She recognised the moment when Alfie noticed the look of guilt that flashed across her face and knew that something was terribly wrong.

'Lexi?' he asked carefully, when she didn't answer David's questions. Lexi tried and failed to find a suitable explanation for what she had done.

'It's okay,' she said suddenly in a surprisingly unwavering voice, moving quickly and looking beyond them into the corridor. She held a hand in front of the security guard as he rushed into the room, looking out of breath and indignant at his territory being invaded. Thinking on her feet,

Lexi tried to find a solution to the destruction she had created around her.

She looked at David and saw he was frightened for the first time and the anger she felt for him melted away in an instant. She finally realised what she really always known – she had been played for a fool by Dr Cole. She felt her cheeks burn red and hot with shame.

Alfie came over and took her into his arms as she started to shake. He gave the security guard a stern look as it seemed as if he was about to start a tirade about what they were doing there, but that one glance silenced him immediately. Eyeing the muscles on David's arms, the security guard obviously decided that picking a fight with these two wasn't worth messing up his pretty face for.

'Have they hurt you?' Alfie demanded of Lexi, looking at her face and into her eyes. Lexi felt her dreams shatter as she realised how futile her crush on Alfie had been. He was peering at her with real concern and friendship, but not lust or passion. She saw how hurtful her actions had probably been to Stacey, and how disrespectful too. She felt utmost certainty, now, that the others would not intentionally hurt or demean her either. She had let her old anger raise its ugly head and consume her, and she had almost dragged everyone down with her.

She felt disgusted by herself and her stomach churned in humiliation that she had been taken in by Dr Cole's lies. She brushed away the tears that were falling haphazardly down her face and, breaking away from Alfie, looked straight at David, who appeared like he was about to burst a fuse with impatience.

The security guard had quietly located his radio and was trying to whisper into it without anyone noticing. Lexi grabbed his arm to stop him. 'It's okay,' she laughed, although the sound came out in a high-pitched squeak. 'I came to speak to Dr Cole as I thought I might be pregnant and he's a good friend of my mother.' This seemed to explain a lot to the receptionist, whose mouth had been open as if, for the life of her, she couldn't understand how a ragamuffin like this would even know the name of Dr Cole. 'It seems like it was a false alarm,' she soothed. David and Alfie looked really confused now and both turned to Lexi for an explanation of what she was playing at. 'This is my brother,' she said pointing to Alfie, 'and his friend,' she continued. 'They have obviously just found out who I was going to speak to and were worried about what I was going to do. I've spoken to Dr Cole and it seems I made a mistake. I'm so embarrassed that they came rushing down here and upset you all.' She pretended to glare at Alfie under her tears. The security guard leant backwards to speak to the receptionist and when she nodded they both gave Lexi a stern look and quickly retreated from the room.

'I'm sorry if I've wasted your time,' Lexi said to Dr Cole's secretary who was still standing by the doorway. 'Would it be okay for me to have that Cola now?' she asked sweetly. The secretary turned wordlessly and brought the tray into the room, setting it carefully down before frowning and starting to speak. Lexi quickly cut her off. 'Do you mind if I talk privately with my brother, now? It can't have been easy for him today and Dr Cole left me a while ago so that I could have some time alone. I actually wanted this baby,' she lied, getting a bit too into her story now and receiving a reproving frown from David, who still looked like he wanted to punch someone.

The secretary sighed and Lexi bet she was wondering why Dr Cole worked in such a fancy office if he hung around with people like them. Lexi hoped that if she thought about buzzing his other office, she wouldn't fancy explaining why she had disturbed a family friend. Lexi almost giggled to herself for a second because now his staff might think that although Dr Cole appeared to have it all worked out, he still had a few skeletons in his closet with friends like them. Perhaps they'd think he had a secret gangster past. She smirked to herself, then realised that they were all staring at her curiously. She quickly straightened her face and cleared her throat as the secretary politely left the room, closing the door behind her.

Once they were alone in the office, David slammed his fist into the desk, making them all jump. Alfie reached out to steady his arm as they didn't want David making the hot secretary rush back in. It had taken them what seemed like ages, but was probably nearer to a few minutes, to get her to stop gawking at them and leave the room. Lexi guessed they didn't usually have boxers and deadbeats hanging around there. *David was actually dressed quite smartly today*, she thought, but she and Alfie surely could do with a brush-up.

'What did you tell them, Lexi?' David demanded to know, as he began pacing the room. His nervous energy made Lexi feel sick. She knew he would require all the details of what she had done to be able to act, and the fact that she was there was a definite red flag. She had said or meddled in something that didn't concern her. One wrong move and Tilly could be hurt, because of her, she now realised.

'Nothing,' she cried in earnest, hating the pain that she could clearly see on David's face. 'I did come here to tell him,' she admitted, imploring him to look at her and understand, but he was just standing stock-still and staring at the walls. 'I'm sorry!' she tried again. 'I'm not perfect like you, David,' she saw him flinch at that. 'I can't keep my emotions in check all the time and I was hurting.' This seemed to resonate with David and he reached out and pulled Lexi into a fierce hug, almost squashing her arms and making her squeak in pain, not comfort, until he realised and let her go.

'I'm not perfect, Lexi,' he said carefully. 'I've just learnt over the years how to control my emotions. A boxer can't show his fear, and neither can a child who is faced with a drunken father who is spoiling for a fight, where the slightest sign of weakness would be seen as an invitation for a blow to the side of the head.'

Lexi shrank away from David in horror. 'I didn't know about your father,' she cried, tears pouring down her face suddenly. She felt her heart would break for the younger David, as well as the man he was now. Alfie came over and hugged her too. 'What happened?' he asked gently. 'Where's Tilly?'

'She's here somewhere,' Lexi sobbed. 'Dr Cole seemed like he was expecting someone else as well. He was agitated and kept looking at his watch. Tilly has been coming here every week,' she explained to David whilst wiping tears from her face.

David looked like he had been slapped and he grabbed on to the nearest chair for support. 'Tilly said she just spoke to him at EVE, and on the phone most of the time!'

Lexi took a deep breath and told David the truth. 'She's been bleeding. She made me swear not to tell you!' she said in a tiny voice when she saw the fire in his eyes. 'I found out by mistake and she thought it would just worry you.'

'Too right it would worry me!' raged David. 'How the hell could she lie to my face like that?'

'Dr Cole has a way of manipulating the situation,' implored Lexi. 'It wasn't Tilly's fault! He told her it would make you stressed when you already had enough to do worrying about everyone at EVE. He told her he could help her if she kept it quiet, or his bosses would give him a rollicking too, for doing too much.' She angrily brushed the tears from her face with the back of her hand and hung her head. 'Dr Cole tricked me too,' she continued. 'He said you'd all used me and laughed about me behind my back, because of my stupid crush on Alfie,' she continued to stare at the floor and couldn't meet Alfie's eyes. Alfie had the good grace to look embarrassed when she chanced a peek upwards and David gave him a harsh, 'I told you so' stare.

'Why would we laugh at you, Lexi?' David asked gently, turning her face to look up at him. 'Everybody in the world has a crush on Alfie!' he tried to joke. Lexi glanced up gratefully and squeezed Alfie's hand, to show him that there were no hard feelings. He squeezed back a little too hard and almost made her cry again.

'I came here with Tilly before, when she had a consultation about her pregnancy,' she continued quickly before David burst a blood vessel. 'Dr Cole called her earlier today about some test results and I heard the call. I followed her here after I found this in your office.' She handed him a business card that she had found on the desk.

David looked down at Tilly's beautiful handwriting and saw that she had written the time and date of the meeting with Dr Cole and a note to herself on the back of the card, to remember to talk to David that evening. David hastily put the card in his pocket and waited for Lexi to continue. 'Dr Cole said that Tilly had told him what was going on at EVE and that he could help Tilly better if I told him more. I'm sure he was lying. Tilly wouldn't do that.'

'Help with the bleeding?' he asked, blatantly trying to keep his voice level, but failing miserably.

'Yes,' Lexi said quietly.

'Why didn't you tell me?' exploded David, seeming not to care now if the stupid staff all came in to see him strangle a teenager. Lexi blanched and felt like she was going to be sick. She looked to Alfie for support, but he appeared livid too as his mouth was set into a grim line. She started to quake in her shoes. She had never been on the wrong side of these two before and it wasn't a nice experience. She tried to settle her nerves. 'I told you before,' she stuttered slightly in anguish. 'Tilly pleaded with me not to,' she said apologetically.

'Why are you still here, if Dr Cole has left?' asked Alfie.

'He wouldn't let me go. He said I had to wait here for Tilly, but I don't think he's coming back. I've been really scared.' She looked at Alfie, imploring him to understand. He led her over to a seat and sat her down. 'You should have trusted us,' was all he said. Her cheeks burned in shame and she hung her head.

'I know,' she replied. 'Dr Cole has been playing me. He said that Tilly needs a confidant, someone she could trust. He said Tilly was unsure you would cope with being a father, David, as you were under so much pressure already with looking after all of us,' she looked up to see a glint of fire come into his eyes. 'He said Stacey hated me and was out to cause me trouble. He said you were a player, Alfie, who was using me for your own amusement.' Alfie just threw his hands up in the air in defeat.

'David's been right the whole time. I've hurt you and Stacey, and you both deserve an apology. Or in Stacey's case, something sparkling and expensive!' he flinched when Lexi flushed. 'I'm sorry if I led you on in some way Lexi.'

'You didn't,' she said simply, her hands curling together in her lap.

'Do you know where Tilly is?' David demanded to

know. He had been patient enough, but Tilly was liable to give birth any time now and Lexi knew that he wasn't going to leave her alone with Dr Cole ever again. He would probably talk to Lexi later, about how stupid she had been, but he would do that after he knew that his girlfriend and baby were safe. Lexi didn't like the atmosphere of this place and the feeling was getting worse by the minute. Her senses were telling her to get out and not to look back.

'The next building along is a medical facility. I looked out of the door as he left and saw him go in. I asked the receptionist what was further along, as I was trying to find a way out. She said it's where they manufacture their pharmaceuticals.' David reached into his pocket and pulled out a security pass.

'What the...!' said Alfie.

'I procured it from Dr Cole's security detail the last time they were at EVE. I thought it might come in handy if we needed to get in and find out what they really want with us.' Alfie laughed and slapped his friend on the back.

'You always manage to surprise me, my friend. Let's go!'

CHAPTER 47

Teddy stepped into the cool interior of his chauffeur-driven car and told his driver the address of the clinic. He didn't look surprised when Jemima opened the door and coolly ducked her head and sat down beside him. He had told her that he had a new respect for her after today and she felt satisfaction course through her body. She wasn't just something pretty to hang onto a powerful man's arm. She was the youngest daughter of Edward Venner and it was about time that people began treating her with the respect she deserved. She was bored with having her face plastered all over the gossip magazines. She wanted to be admired for her brain and not just her looks. Then she could crush men like Lucas and they wouldn't dare to treat her the way he had. They could send Lucas away and she would file for a divorce. Not before tying him up in paperwork for months so that he couldn't work again or utter a word about being her former husband, though.

Her father moved over slightly to make room for her, even though there was enough room for several people in the car's plush interior. He squeezed her knee and smiled reassuringly into her eyes in a totally uncharacteristic show of paternal affection. Jem was seething inside. Not only had her father known about Lucas's dirty little secret, but he had thought his daughter's virtue so trivial, that he had let it go on without telling her. If this had been someone slighting her father, the offender's balls would have been chopped off long ago, but Lucas was still walking around like a proud peacock with his little harem of women, the bastard!

Her father was actually smiling as well, as if all this was his grand plan and that he was the master of all these minions. He was the puppet master, directing his work-force, bending them to his will. She hated him. He didn't want her to be happy. He wanted her to be as evil and manipulative as him.

Nothing she did right would ever please him, only what she could do wrong. She could see that now. She had been a complete fool all these years. He didn't want a doting daughter, he wanted a chip off the old block; a murderous scumbag, who would stand where Daddy Dearest had stood before. She would show him not to underestimate her again.

A glint of ice came into her eyes as she saw her father's admiration as he really looked at her for the first time in her life. Her mind was whizzing with ways to handle this situa-tion. Lucas was dead to her now anyway, but her father? She had spent her whole life trying to make him notice her, when all along she could have just threatened someone and he would have been panting like a dog at her feet in seconds. She wondered idly if she could actually be like her father. Could she murder someone in cold blood, just because they stepped over an imaginary line she had drawn in the sand? Then she thought of the little brown mouse and her belly swollen full of Lucas's child and realised that, if ever there was a time when she would see pride shine in her father's face, it would be the day she wrapped her hands around the neck of the woman who had knowingly stolen her husband and incubated his child.

CHAPTER 48

The government agent sitting vigilantly, pretending to be relaxing with a takeaway coffee on a nearby bench, had seen David and Alfie enter the building and alerted his colleagues who were waiting in a shiny black Mercedes to his right. It was pretty nondescript amongst the prestigious cars in the clinic car park, waiting to burst into life when their owners returned. To all intents and purposes, Gale and her partner looked like any other couple sitting nervously in their car before plucking up the courage to walk to their appointment at the fertility clinic to see one of the revered specialists inside the building.

This was supposed to be one of the country's foremost facilities, but it was the building alongside it that had Gale's attention. She had been following Dr Cole's career for years and unobtrusively infiltrating his files, using his work to assist her own. His employer thought he was above the law and that he could manipulate anyone to his own end. He was about to find out how wrong that way of thinking was.

She quickly told her own employers about the development of the two men arriving. They had been listening to

Dr Cole try and coerce the young girl called Lexi into sharing information with him. Gale held her breath in nervous anticipation of the girl saying something, but she had backed away from his clumsy questioning and clammed up completely. Gale couldn't blame her. Dr Cole's interrogation techniques were archaic! No wonder the teenager had run a mile, or tried to, before being subtly held in his office with a promise of seeing her pregnant friend. That had been his only smart move.

The airwaves crackled to life. Jackpot! A vehicle with blacked out windows was entering the car park. The minute it ground to a halt in front of the clinic not only Teddy Venner, but his stunning daughter too, got out and walked up to the medical centre. Gale frowned. What was the daughter doing here? She usually just sat around looking pretty and seducing hapless pool guys. Gale looked at Jem again and quickly relayed the details of this development to her backup teams. This could mess everything up and she swore under her breath, whilst quickly calculating what this meant for her plan, and how she could use it to benefit her own employer.

Jem didn't look happy to Gale, but her father was being very solicitous, waiting for her to precede him into the building, which went against the normal behaviour that Gale had become quite familiar with on this case. 'Hold back!' she hissed into the mouthpiece. She didn't want this change of plan to compromise months and months of hard work. A few more minutes could make the world of difference to the outcome.

As soon as Teddy Venner and his daughter were safely inside the building, Gale spoke to her team about the latest development and then she told them what she wanted them to do.

CHAPTER 49

David, Alfie and Lexi quietly opened the door and saw that the receptionist had taken them at their word and given them some privacy. She was probably loitering somewhere nearby, though, so they didn't want to risk alerting her to their actions. They quietly moved further into the building, towards the door Lexi had seen Dr Cole go through.

David pulled the security card out of his pocket and ran it through the entry box by the door until it turned green and the door soundlessly slid open. He glanced at Lexi, who looked like her heart would burst in her chest from fright when the door opened, but he could see she was pressing her nails into her palms to stop herself from letting David and Alfie down again. He could not let her ruin this for them. They needed to find Tilly. There was definitely more going on here than just a place that made food supplements, as far as he could see. David grabbed Lexi's hand and motioned to Alfie to follow him to the left, where there was a large sterile room which looked like an operating theatre. There were huge photos on the walls of breathtaking sea scenes, which David guessed were to create a relaxed environment, but they felt at odds with the purpose of the room. He felt his blood boil when he realised that Dr Cole was in the next room along, which was partitioned off by sound-proof glass, and he was leaning over the still form of a woman.

Alfie frantically grabbed David's arm to hold him back, but David was too fast for him and his hand was around Dr Cole's throat within seconds, stopping what he was about to do.

Tilly started to moan quietly while Dr Cole gasped and his eyes boggled as he tried desperately to find air with David's fingers on his windpipe. His arms flailed around helplessly and he spluttered in alarm at the unexpected intrusion. 'No one is supposed to be allowed in here. How the hell did you get in?' he croaked before David's piercing eyes met his and he must have realised that he really couldn't breathe. His body went rigid and his leg, which was by now off the floor, hit Tilly's and she groaned in pain. She looked like she had been drugged and was barely coher-ent, but the noise registered with David and he dropped Dr Cole to the floor, where he cowered like a wounded animal.

David tried to take control of his emotions when he saw Tilly lying there. He wanted to rip Dr Cole's head from his shoulders. He shot Dr Cole a warning glare that told him not to move and Alfie walked over to bar his way out from the side of the bed. Lexi ran over to Tilly and grabbed her hand, chanting her name over and over again, trying to get her to wake up.

'What have you done to her?' raged David, losing all control now and wanting to kill someone for what they had done to his beautiful Tilly. She looked so small and helpless lying there and she had blood smeared all over the top of her legs, just below the cream hospital tunic she was wearing.

Dr Cole grasped his throat and tried to control his breathing. He frantically looked around the room, but David felt a frisson of satisfaction when Dr Cole saw that there was no way out of this one for him. Alfie was barring his escape and David knew he looked as if he would gladly kill him with his bare hands if he so much as looked at him the wrong way. 'You must let me help her,' Dr Cole pleaded.

'Help her? Look what you've done to her!' said Alfie with a sharp edge to his voice, glancing behind him to make sure no one had followed them.

'My nurse has just gone to get some blood,' Dr Cole whimpered. 'I wanted to find out how your girls are getting pregnant, when it's so hard for normal women.'

'Normal women!' said Lexi scathingly. 'What do you think we are, freaks?'

'That's the point,' said Dr Cole witheringly in her direction. 'There must be something freakish about you, as you all keep getting pregnant! What is it? A super stud who holds the future of our race in his hands? A cult?' He waved his hands round in frustration at coming so close to realising his life's work, and seemed to forget the precarious position he was in for a moment before he glanced up and met David's eye. He gulped in some more air and continued meekly. 'Teddy Venner has threatened to cut me in half if I don't uncover the reason for the drop in our population. It has been so dramatic, but it seems that the women at your warehouse just have to look at a sperm to get pregnant. I needed a newborn blood sample,' he whined.

'From my child?' roared David grabbing hold of Dr

Cole by the shirt collar and hoisting him to his feet. Dr Cole's legs were so shaky that he almost fell down again.

'You could have killed her!' shouted David, not caring now who heard him. He reached out with his free hand to take Tilly's and tried to calm down before he did something stupid, like pick her up and run out of there. She didn't look like she was in any state to be moved and the blood on her legs was making him feel like he needed to vomit.

'No really! I wouldn't have... well, probably not,' stuttered Dr Cole. 'I only needed some blood, not all of it, and most newborns can handle a little blood loss.'

'But not all of them?' Lexi asked in a whisper.

'Some may get a little jaundice or have a slight iron deficiency.' Dr Cole's voice quivered with nerves. 'I would have given Tilly details of how to deal with the conditions afterwards.'

David looked down at the pathetic heap of a man. 'Without letting her know you were the cause of it,' he spat. Dr Cole shrank further and tried to hide behind the medical equipment by the side of the bed that was now beeping loudly.

'Mr Venner gave me no choice,' he pleaded, staring imploringly at Lexi for understanding. She cussed under her breath and ignored him, jumping up as the machine squealed and scared the living daylights out of her.

'Tilly!' cried David, grasping her hand and trying to wake her up. She seemed to have drifted into a dreamless sleep and was barely moving now. Her swollen eyelids began to close and she had a small smile on her lips, as if she had just discovered something wonderful and was keeping it as a surprise.

'Help her!' screamed Lexi, sobbing now as Alfie pulled her away and took her in his arms as her body shook with fear. Dr Cole leapt into action and pressed a red button which sounded an emergency call. 'No-one but my most trusted team are usually allowed into this private theatre,' he said, but on hearing the siren four more people rushed in from a corridor on the other side of the room and they all crowded round the bed. David was pushed away from Tilly and into the nearest wall.

The nurse from earlier arrived with fresh blood and was about to set up the drip into Tilly's arm, when her eyes flew open. 'No!' she cried, throwing her arms wide and almost knocking out two of the medical team, who ducked and stared in shock at the fact that she had woken up so dramatically. David shoved them out of the way and gave them all a warning look and they backed away slightly to give him room.

Tilly looked into David's eyes as she cried out in pain and began to brace her legs and push down through her pelvis. David grabbed her hand and smiled into her eyes, trying to control his emotions and not scare the hell out of her as she seemed unaware of what was happening to her. Dr Cole burst into action and started checking on Tilly's vital signs and, along with the nurse, they looked to see if this was what they thought it was. Somehow, Tilly's labour had started.

'The baby's head is crowning,' whispered the nurse to Dr Cole. 'She's fully dilated and the baby's coming.'

She looked up and smiled at David reassuringly. She looked pointedly at David. 'I need the dad on side to calm the atmosphere. I'm used to frantic fathers with my job in the main clinic, dealing with the IVF parents who have often waited such a heartbreakingly long time to meet their children. It's very rare to have a day like today, when Dr Cole is actually delivering the child. If you are staying in this room, then you need to let us do our job and deliver the baby safely.'

She gestured for some of the staff to clear the room and gave one quick nod to her colleagues. They tried to draw Alfie and Lexi from the room with them. Some of the staff still looked confused at having rushed to an emergency, then not being needed after all.

'Most of them have rarely been into this theatre before,' said the nurse, obviously trying to distract David from Tilly's wails of pain. 'They have heard rumours that only royalty get to come in here to give birth,' she looked him up and down and then seemed to dismiss him from that line of thinking. 'I haven't seen a Royal here myself, but I keep hoping. The staff are allowed in this room for advanced training, but otherwise it's kept empty, which seems a complete waste of a perfectly good theatre,' she rambled on, while David just wanted her to shut up and concentrate on Tilly.

The nurse leant in to assist Dr Cole and the remaining staff seemed to snap out of their reverie and rushed to help, grabbing trays of medical instruments and hovering nearby. One gently started to clean some of the blood away from Tilly's legs, whilst another handed over some sort of metal tongs to the nurse, who used them to ease the baby's way into the world. David held tightly on to Tilly's hand as she tried to sit up, then gave an almighty roar and pushed down with all her might to get the baby out. She seemed only dimly aware of David whispering in her ear, telling her she was wonderful and that she would be the best mum in the world. She mumbled that her baby needed her and she was confused about where she was, before zoning out again.

David looked at the woman who was gently wiping the blood from Tilly's legs. 'What about all the blood loss?' he asked the nurse, completely ignoring Dr Cole, who was darting from Tilly to the medical trolley, checking the vital signs for her and the baby every few seconds. 'Does she need more blood?'

'The baby has come just in time,' said Dr Cole shiftily, before the nurse could speak. She glanced at him in surprise, then carried on assisting the birth. The baby's head was almost all the way out now, and one more push and this little boy or girl could be placed into its mother arms. Tilly gave one more scream and almost split David's fingers in half with the pressure of her own hands and he yelped in pain. The nurse smiled for the first time and a wail hit the air. Not from Tilly this time, but from the new baby boy who had just been delivered into the world.

Tilly's eyes roamed around the room in confusion, then focused on David and she gave him an almost serene smile. He had never seen her look so ethereal and he glanced down as the nurse took the baby to be weighed and cleaned before placing him on Tilly's chest. David had not let his child out of his sight and slumped down on a chair that one of the medical staff had brought over, and stared at his girl-friend and child in shock.

The midwife was still checking Tilly's pulse and scribbling notes on a chart, before quietly moving away to speak to Dr Cole, who David could see was by now trying to work out how he could extract himself from this mess. He signalled for all of the other staff to leave the room and they rapidly did his bidding. Dr Cole looked at the outline of Alfie outside the theatre door, so he knew that there was no way he could get out that way. His nurse interrupted his train of thought and was quite insistent that he listen to her, even though he was her boss. He mumbled that she should bloody well do what she was told and shut up. David heard her ask if Tilly did need the blood transfusion she had set up, because she had lost a fair amount of blood earlier. It had been a small haemorrhage and nowhere near the baby, but still, surely it was better to be safe than sorry. The girl had just given birth and would be wiped out by that alone.

Dr Cole darted a glance at David. Fear was etched on his face over how he could explain the blood loss. The doctor stuttered, but then threw his arms up in frustration. 'The blood around Tilly's legs isn't hers,' he confessed. 'I needed the extra blood to be on standby and by making it look like she was bleeding, it was easier to explain away. We have been waiting patiently to test the blood of women in labour to try and find the cause of the defective gene that is rendering so many women infertile. I wasn't sure how much I would need to take.' The nurse looked stunned, horrified and confused, but one look from her employer and she was silenced. 'I gave Tilly a sedative just after she started to push, which isn't ideal... but she was getting a bit hysterical about you not being there, so I had to react quickly.' David moved towards him, his fists bunching, but he glanced at Tilly and stood still.

Dr Cole put his hands up in surrender. 'Look, It maybe wasn't my best idea ever, as it could have hurt the baby, but my research was nearly complete. This could help so many other women.' He took a look at the contented baby, who did look a bit dozy, and he crumpled into a chair. 'It was only a gentle sedative and I got so near to my goal of solving this mystery that I now feel I may have gone a bit mad. The sedative was mild, but I had to stop her pushing the baby out for a while. The drug might have crossed over into the baby's bloodstream. I could have killed them both,' he said in despair. 'What the hell is happening to me? I used to be a family man myself before I met Teddy Venner.' Dr Cole put his head in his hands and signalled to his nurse to check on Tilly, so she quickly scurried past him, looking terrified. 'Once I realised the depth of my boss's cruelty, it was too late to wrest myself from his influence.'

'And you expect me to feel sorry for you?' asked David.

'It was made clear that my family was in danger other-wise,' whined Dr Cole. 'I felt it was safer to leave them completely. The look in my daughter's eyes, and the tears she cried as I left, broke my heart. Over the years, the pain of losing them should have lessened, but it's just got steadily worse. I have nothing left in my life now but my research. I hoped I could help my own daughter have a child if this was a global problem. I've become a desperate man.'

David was distracted for a moment by movement from his precious baby, and Alfie was comforting the worried teenager, so Dr Cole jumped up to make his escape and to finally break free from MAZE. He felt along the wall for a hidden handle that led to a small corridor out of the theatre at the back, just as David noticed what he was doing and sprang forward.

The door was shoved open before Dr Cole could pull it and Teddy Venner stepped into the room with his daughter, Jemima, at his side.

CHAPTER 50

Teddy glared at Dr Cole, who visibly shrank back and quickly moved towards David for protection. Even though David looked like he wanted to murder him too, Dr Cole probably thought that he was a safer bet than Teddy, although the fact that he was there, and they had all seen him, didn't really bode well for any of them getting out of the room alive. Jemima's presence was possibly the only fly in the plan Teddy was quickly calculating for them.

Jem gasped in shock when she saw Tilly and her baby. She groped for her dad's arm to support her. 'Dad?' she asked. 'What are these people doing here?' Tilly scooped her baby protectively against her chest and he let out a little squeak of protest, before falling back to sleep almost immediately. David stood in front of them menacingly. Alfie barged into the room, and squared his shoulders for a fight when he saw David standing in front of Tilly's bed, blocking her from harm. Alfie's huge frame seemed to fill the room and make it smaller and Teddy quickly surmised what was going on. Dr Cole had messed up again. Teddy hadn't expected these two goons to be there, but as long as

Dr Cole had the samples he needed, then perhaps the men could be left unaware of what had happened and how close they had all come to disappearing permanently.

Teddy glared at Dr Cole and, grasping his lapel, hissed into his ear, 'Did you get the samples?' making Dr Cole shrink further away and start stuttering a grovelling apology.

'No!' said David clearly. 'He didn't take any blood from my girlfriend or my baby.'

Jem looked at her father in confusion. Blood rushed to Teddy's face and he looked at Dr Cole accusingly. The pathetic man hunched down in defeat. Teddy straightened up and patted Jem's hand on his arm. He would take care of Dr Cole later. The man had used up all of his free passes and was headed for a small black hole in the ground.

'Dad?' said Jem again, looking round as if trying to understand what on earth they were doing in a room with these huge men and a woman with her very tiny-looking baby. Tilly curved her arms protectively around her child and David curled his hands into fists, ready to strike. He conveyed in one look to Teddy Venner the fact that he knew what the older man had tried to do to his family and that there would be repercussions.

Teddy had dealt with many men like David and Alfie in his time and wasn't afraid of them; that emotion seemed to have left him years ago. All he felt now was a cold annoyance that Dr Cole had failed him and that Jem was witnessing this mess. If only Dr Cole had managed to get the samples before this motley crew arrived, then perhaps they wouldn't know the full story and he could get around this problem. Now things were getting messy and he couldn't afford for Jem to see him doing the actual dirty work himself. He didn't want her to think he was a monster, but the situation at hand was complicated by the number of people in the room that now knew what he had been looking for.

Dr Cole shrank away from his boss's venomous glare and started stuttering apologies, his head bowed in submission. Teddy restrained himself from kicking Dr Cole in his snivelling face, but only just. *No matter*, he thought to himself, reining in his emotions with a practiced air, he would deal with the incompetent employee after he had got the results he wanted.

Teddy turned to Jem and smiled, as if he didn't have a care in the world. He placed a hand on her arm and moved her subtly to the back of the room near to the door. This hadn't been how he was expecting today to end, and it was annoying, but he didn't really see it as too much of an issue. He itched to take them all out with the handgun he always carried, but having his daughter there posed a problem. These down and outs were all a bit thick anyway and would buy any bullshit he gave them. If not, he could probably pay them off until he could discreetly find another solution.

'These people have been helping me with a little experiment, Jem,' he soothed. 'It's nothing to concern yourself with.' He tried to shut her questioning down with a smile and a subtle look, but she was ignoring him and stamping her heels as usual. Maybe it had been a mistake to bring her along. He had thought she would be there to witness his crowning glory and share his hopes for the future, but maybe he had misjudged her and she was just the annoying, incompetent child he had always taken her for.

Teddy thought of his team of professional cleaners who tidied up any mess he made, making sure that there was no physical trace of the bodies left behind. He had sent them earlier to collect Lucas and that insipid girl he had got pregnant, and he wondered where the hell they were? They would have to sort out the confusion Dr Cole had created, too, and that would be harder to explain away. Looking at the redhead and her slumbering baby, the scruffy teenager and her minder, the tall black guy, he sighed. Perhaps it was good that Jem was here. He would find out if she had the stomach to handle his daily life. Things were starting to get boringly repetitive with Dr Cole – the constant messes he had to clean up. He would have to check out the staff situation too and see who had been around that night and how they could explain things away without too many casualties.

'We weren't helping you,' said David slowly, making everyone in the room turn and stare at his commanding presence. He turned to Jem and his demeanour demanded she listen to him. She looked confused as if she was still trying to take in what was going on.

Teddy felt his irritation grow by the minute and Jemima darted a look around the room and her hands began to shake. A bead of sweat ran down the side of her face and she angrily brushed it away.

'Your father decided that he would use us as his lab rats without telling us. Do we look like lab rats?' David asked Jem, his voice steely and his arms crossed in front of his impressive chest. Jem darted another look at her father and then to the baby in Tilly's arms and her face paled.

'Daddy?' she asked again. 'Is the drop in the population something to do with you? Are you the reason that Lucas and I couldn't have a baby?' she shrieked hysterically.

'Don't be so dramatic, Jemima!' scolded Teddy in exasperation at his daughter's outburst. The girl really was silly after all. He felt his earlier equilibrium deflate, like a balloon left in the corner after an all-night party.

Tilly tried to heave herself off the bed and shook her

head as if she was attempting to clear the fug inside her brain. She had been trying to focus on what was happening around her, but seemed like she couldn't quite grasp what was going on. She frowned in concentration. 'Why is my baby so sleepy?' she mumbled groggily. 'I'm exhausted and my tummy hurts.' David quickly turned round and eased Tilly back on to the bed, plumping up the pillows and resting her head on them. She let out a weary sigh and seemed to drift off to sleep again, before snapping her eyes open and looking around at everyone in the room in confusion.

Jem stepped into her eyeline and raged at her father, making Tilly wince and the baby start to cry, before she hushed and rocked him gently. 'There's a baby involved,' Jem screamed, before lowering her voice at the sound of the baby's cries. Anger blazed through Teddy. He knew she would turn out to be weak after all. The disappointment was crushing and he was surprised to realise that he didn't actually care now about what Jem thought.

'Oh, it was okay for you to torture Lucas and take his baby from Poppy, but this baby is different?' he sneered. Jem shrank back a little as the venom in her father's voice hit her right in the chest. David and the others looked at Jem in shock and she could see the disgust they felt clearly on their faces. Her bloody father!

'He's my husband and that bitch stole him. She's pregnant with his baby.' She stamped her feet like the spoilt child she was and her eyes flamed with anger and hatred at the years of hurt her father had put her through. 'I wanted him to feel some of the pain he had made me feel. I was never actually going to harm the little dormouse or her bastard child!'

'Even if you desperately wanted to,' sneered Teddy.

'I felt for a few moments what it was like to bask in the warmth of your praise,' she yelled at him, 'but the cost is just too high. I'm not a murderer,' she blazed at her father. 'Unlike you!' She was becoming hysterical now.

Tilly pulled her baby protectively to her chest and tried to soothe his muffled cries before David scooped him into his arms and passed him to Alfie, telling him to get Tilly and Lexi out of there quickly. Teddy could see that Jem meant business and that she had been cornered and wouldn't back down. Jem turned, manically grabbing a sharp cutting tool from the medical supply desk behind her, as all of the pent up tears and aggression began to surge forward. She swung her arm round, ready to strike her father. Years of mental abuse and neglect had boiled together into a melting pot of uncontrollable rage and she lunged and screamed that she wanted it to end now.

As her arm swung to strike, a hand reached out and caught her arm, whilst Teddy gasped in horror and ducked away from this hideous creature of his own making. 'Is this violent enough for you, Daddy?' she asked, making the baby whimper and Tilly start to cry, where Alfie and Lexi were trying to heave her out of the bed.

Jem seemed vaguely aware through her fog of anger that she wasn't moving, and looked to see what was restraining her. She seemed confused to see a swarm of bodies fill the room and she tried to dart her head around to see where her father had gone.

The girl holding one of her arms was slight, the man holding the hand with the knife was the huge blond man, who was looking down on her with pity. Her anger left her as suddenly as it had arrived and she slumped down on to the floor and sobbed for the childhood she had never had. She glanced round to where her father was being restrained. 'You're not worthy of my love,' she sobbed. 'You deserve nothing but scorn. You live life draining the power from others to make yourself feel good, when in reality you're so weak that you have to leech from everyone else. You aren't someone to admire, you're someone to revile. I hate you!'

Teddy was angrily trying to shake off the men who had taken hold of him and were cuffing his wrists. He started to spin them a line about this being Dr Cole's research lab, and he and his daughter had stumbled into something sinister. His daughter had been protecting herself and him...

Dr Cole was being handcuffed to a young police officer and looked almost relieved that this was finally all over, until he realised that he was being led away with Teddy, who still wanted to murder him.

CHAPTER 51

David leant over and gave Gale a big hug, once she had handed Jem over to her colleague. 'Hi, Gale,' said Tilly sleepily, still trying to get herself off the side of the bed with both Alfie and Lexi grappling on to her. Alfie had her slumbering baby in one arm and was trying to help her up with the other, whilst all the drama unfolded around him. She was so slippery, though, and she just kept flopping back down onto the bed. Lexi hadn't managed to grab a firm hold of her either, and she was still trying to work out if she was terrified or elated that the police were there and arresting that hysterical woman and her mad father. The woman had seemed like she wanted to slice her father to pieces, but Alfie was always saying that the apple didn't fall far from the tree, whatever that meant. They were all fit for the looney bin. Finally, who the hell was Gale?

Alfie handed the baby to David, who gently took his son in his arms and stared at him in awe. Gale smiled at the little bundle in his arms and gave him the softest kiss on his cheek. Alfie leant in and gave Gale a hug too, making Lexi even more confused. Why was everyone hugging the little policewoman?

'What are you doing here?' Alfie asked Gale. 'I should have known that David would never have risked Tilly or his baby by barging in there and hoping for the best. I thought his plan seemed a bit vague!' he joked, giving his friend a pat on the back for having the whole thing sorted from the start.

No wonder he had been fairly relaxed throughout, thought Lexi, *except when he had had to react quickly and disarm the madwoman. She might have been bonkers, but she was totally stunning!* Lexi had never seen such a beautiful woman in real life. Even Stacy wasn't that pretty.

Gale sent an affectionate smile to Alfie. 'You've been my brother's greatest ally and have got him through some really tough times.' Lexi smirked as it seemed that she wasn't the only one with a soft spot for Alfie. The fact that he was a great big hunk of gorgeousness obviously hadn't gone unnoticed. 'David called me when MAZE started to take an interest in the warehouse centre, and Tilly especially,' she explained, suddenly noticing Lexi who was eyeing her warily from the corner. She smiled at her reassuringly. It was probably part of her job to be a calming influence and she was good at it, noted Lexi, as the atmosphere had changed to something completely different since she'd arrived.

'David knew we had been keeping a close eye on Venner Trading and their subsidiaries for years. We have been known to swap info and help each other out,' she confided quietly for Alfie's ears only, with a wink.

'This time David's instincts were on high alert for some reason. Couldn't be the fact that his whole family were crammed into that warehouse!' she joked, poking him in the ribs and making him squirm, to Lexi's amusement. She had never seen anyone make David uncomfortable before, even with a bit of friendly banter. It was great fun to watch.

'I learnt from the best,' he parried back with a nudge in Gale's direction, almost sending her off her feet. Alfie winked at her, making her laugh and the remaining tension left the room.

Lexi decided she had had enough of all this confusing chat and leaned in to introduce herself, pushing past one of the only two uniformed policemen left in the room who were walking around quietly taking notes. 'I'm Lexi,' she nodded her head to Gale, giving Tilly's arm a quick squeeze on the way past.

'Gale,' said the small woman with sparkly eyes. 'Abbigail,' she sighed and explained, when she saw David give Tilly a dark look. 'I usually drop the Abbie, but David hates it when I do.'

'Abbigail,' said David slowly and clearly, as if speaking to a small child, and earning a quick kick to the shins from his little sister. 'Abbigail was one of the people who helped me to set up EVE. Until the government decided that they required her investigative skills more than I did and squirreled her away to teach her all about catching the bad guys.' He ruffled the top of Abbigail's hair and she ran a hand over the plump arm of the slumbering baby.

'Growing up in our house gave us insider knowledge on understanding how to spot the really bad ones,' she sighed. 'I guess this little guy is my new nephew?' She scooped the baby from David's arms and gave him a quick cuddle. The baby woke with a start and began to cry small mewing sounds, like he wasn't quite sure yet how to use his voice. She shushed and whispered to him and he stopped crying and stared at her in wonder. They had the same piercing blue eyes.

The room was thinning out now and someone came and spoke quietly into Abbigale's ear. 'Sorry, guys,' she said quickly. 'I have to get back and see what these creeps have been storing on their systems. It seems that the world will stop at nothing to find out what is happening with the birth rate. Even stooping so low as to test a baby!' She gave her new family member a firm squeeze and gently handed him back to Tilly, who was now sitting back on the bed and gradually starting to look more like herself, albeit someone that had been through a mangle and spat out the other side.

'What on earth has been going on, David?' she asked in confusion. 'What are Alfie and Lexi and, more to the point, all these people, and your sister, doing in my labour suite? Did they all watch me give birth?' she queried, her mouth dropping open in horror. 'Is our baby okay?' she clutched him to her chest and he squeaked in protest, before she released him a little.

David sighed and walked over to the side of the bed. He sat down and cuddled his new family to him. 'I'll explain everything later, when we all get out of here.'

'What about Poppy?' said Alfie.

'Who the hell is Poppy?' asked Lexi, throwing her arms up into the air in exasperation.

CHAPTER 52

Poppy stared at her own child, a little girl, with complete awe and wonder. 'We did it!' she whispered to Lucas. 'We made this beautiful baby girl.' Tears fell down her face and Lucas gently wiped them away with his own hands. He felt like his chest was going to burst with pride, before his eyes clouded over and he remembered his other family and how they would react to what had happened today.

Teddy was still a real threat to both him and Poppy, and now there was his beautiful daughter to protect too. He felt rage fill his chest and he tried not to look Poppy in the eye as she could read him so easily. She would immediately be on the defensive and start worrying again. For now, she was snuggling up with their daughter and looking blissful as she gave her her first feed. Unless Lucas could bring forward his plans to get away from the cloying suffocation of Teddy and Jem, Poppy and the baby would have to stay in hiding.

Stacey popped her head around the door and smiled when she saw Poppy and the baby. Lucas was glad to see a friendly face, this young girl, whom he had never met before today, but who had been one of the few people to keep him sane. Throughout the ordeal of a fairly quick, but excruciatingly painful, birth for Poppy, Stacey had remained calm and helpful and had not left Lucille's side. He would never judge a person by outer appearances again. Stacey looked like she wouldn't lift a manicured finger even one inch to help anyone, but she had mucked in and she seemed ruffled, but happy. Her dry wit and flashing smile had kept him wide awake and prevented him from throwing himself into a total panic every time Poppy screamed out in pain.

Lucille had handled everything with total aplomb and she was so relaxed that he was surprised she was even awake. It was difficult to panic when everyone around you was a vision of serenity. He glanced at his perfect little daughter with her halo of blond hair, and his beautiful Poppy, who seemed like she didn't have a care in the world now that she had her daughter in her arms, and his resolve hardened. He would leave Jem and turn Teddy over to the authorities. He had been working on this for almost a year now, but had baulked in the middle as his fear of Teddy grew and the pressure had got too much. He had let Poppy down. He should have confided in her, but he had wanted to be her hero and manage the situation on his own. He realised now that he was out of his depth and he had to think quickly.

He had originally been contacted by a government agent called Gale Love. She was a tiny little woman, but she seemed so powerful somehow that he had been impressed. She had managed to ingratiate herself into his group of business contacts and he had noticed her because she always seemed to be watching him and she had the most amazingly bright blue, questioning eyes.

He had finally given in and approached her after one meeting with an associate company, as he was still none the wiser as to who she was. He had been very direct and asked her what she wanted with him. She had thrown her head back and laughed at his audacity, as she had thought she was being quite subtle in her interest in him. He didn't need to know she had used tried and tested techniques to draw his attention her way. She had worn a brighter shade of clothes than the often-used muted palette, favoured by some office workers. She didn't go for red, as that would have set off alarm bells and made her too obvious, but strong shades of blue and green had set her apart from her apparent colleagues and drew his eye to her every time that they met.

He had enquired who she was to his senior staff and was told she was a new associate for a rising sports brand that MAZE was courting. Her laughter had made him smile, but he had drawn in a sharp breath when she had taken him aside to explain her position. She knew her chances of getting him alone would be limited, so she had to make use of the time she had available and move quickly.

It had taken months of negotiation, but in the end it had been surprisingly easy to give her the information that she needed on Teddy. The man was an egotist, who thought he was untouchable! Lucas bringing Poppy into the equation had only hardened his resolve. Originally, he had wanted relief from the pressure Teddy and Jem piled on to him, but recently Poppy had filled that void. That in itself had created a new problem with Teddy but Gale had offered him a way out. She had turned a blind eye to his plans with Teddy's main competitor, to sell Lucas's shares in Venner Trading and buy him and Poppy the freedom to travel and start again somewhere new, and she had offered him an alternative. One where Lucas could help her put Teddy behind bars and then step up to his rightful place as the director of Venner Trading. Teddy would have no choice. There was no one else whom he could trust to run the place, and he knew it. He wouldn't be able to touch Poppy, or Lucas would bring the company down like a house of cards. With Gale's help, Teddy and Jemima would just be a bad memory and Lucas could start afresh with his new family. He would need to be strong to take over Venner Trading, but with Poppy behind him, he felt like he could conquer the world.

CHAPTER 53

Stacey snapped her phone back together and steadied herself on Lucille's immaculately clean kitchen counter. She had just spoken to Alfie, who had excitedly told her that Tilly had given birth to a baby boy. Not only that, but David had managed to get to her in time. He had also jabbered on and on about David and Poppy. She had tried to get him to slow down and speak some sense, but there was a lot of background noise wherever he was and she couldn't hear him clearly. She thought he was explaining about what David said earlier, how Poppy and David were brother and sister, but surely that couldn't be right? He'd said that David's mum was alive and well and had been living with another man and their child. So much for a desperate mother who would never leave her baby. Stacey felt bile rise in the back of her throat. Alfie had often whispered to her about the hours and hours David had spent searching the streets for his mum. Until his dad had put an end to it, that was. She frowned and wondered what Abbigail would make of it all, then remembered Gale's knack of finding out everything anyway, and realised that she probably already knew. No wonder the government had come knocking and offered her that job. How many people from round there got offered a job like that? Especially one they didn't even have to spend years training for. Gale had always had her nose stuck into everything and was a wealth of local information. That's why her friends had nicknamed her 'Gale', because she spun you around and seeped into your bones, finding everything there was to know about you, leaving you stunned and windblown from the experience. How did she do that?

It had come in very useful for David over the years though, and Stacey felt better knowing that David's little sister was keeping an eye out for them all. She was a force to be reckoned with, just like her older brother. Stacey wondered what Poppy was like. Was she a fighter too, like the others? Stacey grabbed some wine glasses out of Lucille's cupboard and scrabbled around until she found a bottle of white wine at the back of the fridge. *Good old Lucille,* she thought. *Always comes up trumps. It's time to celebrate.*

CHAPTER 54

Gale had only been back in the room for about ten minutes, but already she was getting itchy feet. She placed her new nephew back into Tilly's welcoming arms and kissed him softly on the forehead. 'As if your big burly dad would let anyone harm even one hair on your precious little head,' she joked, letting out all of the tension she had felt at having to let her brother walk in there unaided.

David had contacted her some months before and expressed concern about the MAZE group and how they operated, as one of EVE's kids had been working for an accounting firm owned by MAZE for three months prior to the newspaper article. David had helped him find the confidence to apply for the seemingly unreachable role. The job he had been offered had seemed so exciting at the time. None of their kids had worked for a big company like that before. It hadn't taken David long to find out that the company was a subsidiary of MAZE, but the boy had reported back to David that he wasn't happy about a couple of things he had been asked to do, so David had done his own research into the company and how it was run. He wasn't encouraged by what he'd learned and he immediately picked up the phone to Gale.

David's contacts had given him the lowdown on MAZE, but it had been Gale who had the resources to get to Lucas. They made a great team. It was a shame that David didn't want to join her work. She smiled to herself, staring up at the huge hulk that was her big brother. She knew that he had finally found a home and had created his own family. She could understand why he couldn't leave them. Gale had too many barriers up to let a man into her life at the moment, but she hoped that one day they would come down a little and someone would get a chance to vault themselves into the furnace of burning love inside her, if only she would let them in. Her father had made her grow up being incredibly wary of most men and her mother had not exactly been a great role model either. Thank goodness for David, she thought, seeing him smile down at Tilly. Tilly was a lucky girl and the beautiful baby in her arms would grow up in a secure and loving home. Gale felt sad for the two frightened children she and David had been. No wonder David fought every day to make the world a better place for other children.

The newspaper article couldn't have come out at a better time, as it turned out, Gale had explained. Who knew that MAZE would fall slap bang into their laps and drag her brother into the drama too? David had asked Gale to look into the company so that he could rest easier about any of the kids from the warehouse working there; he hadn't been planning on Teddy Venner dragging his family into his sordid little plans for test cases for a new generation.

David scooted along the bed to make room for Gale to sit down next to him and ran his fingers along Tilly's face, kissing her sweetly on the lips and looking glad it was all over. Alfie came up and leant on the metal table at the far side of the bed, bringing Lexi, who was still pale from earlier events, and sitting her down on a white chair next to the bed. 'Whatever happened to a private birth!' joked Tilly, nuzzling her son closely to her and giggling as he blew bubbles from his mouth in response.

Gale got up and scooched everyone who wasn't expressly necessary out of the room. She gave David a warm hug and kissed Tilly. She blew a kiss to Alfie and nodded to Lexi before taking her leave to go and find out where they were holding Teddy and his daughter. Jemima had certainly looked like she wanted to throttle her father earlier and Gale smiled at the thought of all of the juicy information she could squeeze out of her before she ran out of steam.

Hopefully, the little firecracker would rather not have her family's dirty laundry hung out in public and would agree to a deal. She had threatened Poppy and almost killed her own father too. Gale would bet on Jemima giving Lucas his divorce, taking the family money and living out her life somewhere far from here. Hopefully, she would find some peace from the pressure of her father's scorn. Gale could relate to how that felt, she winced. She had met Jem's type before, though, and guessed that she would be shacked up with an overbearing sugar daddy who barely gave her the time of day, before the year was out.

The two nurses left in the room caught Gale's eye and she asked her brother to move to let them check on Tilly and the baby. Alfie and Lexi jumped up too and they all wandered to the back of the room until the nurses took their leave. Even though Teddy Venner's plans seemed to have been curtailed, none of them was leaving anything to chance and would not let Tilly, or the baby, out of their sight until they were safely out of that awful place.

Gale poked her head around the door as the nurses left and winked at Lexi, who gave her a shy smile in return. 'An ambulance is on its way to take you to a proper hospital, before we shut this place down and rip it apart to find out its secrets.'

'They were trying to find out our secrets,' said David, with a sigh.

'They could have just asked!' said Gale cheekily, trying to lighten the atmosphere and let her brother know he wasn't alone in this. He rubbed his forehead with an exhausted hand, looking worried about how Tilly and his son were coping with all the drama. They seemed to have slept through most of it, but Gale knew Tilly and she would want every tiny detail, as soon as they were alone again.

CHAPTER 55

David thought of Poppy, Lucas and their baby. Alfie had told him that Poppy had had a baby girl! He wondered how she would feel having him as a big brother and an amazing, crazy little sister like Abbigail. They came as a package, but he had a sneaking feeling that she would be glad. He grasped Tilly's hand and she squeezed back in support. It had been a harrowing time for all of them. The time would come when he would have to sit down face to face with his mother, too, and see if he could ever understand why she had left him with a violent bully like his father.

He took a deep breath while his son slept on and his friends and family waited for him to tell them what they were going to do next. 'I think we should just go on as before,' he decided levelly. 'Abbigail has told me that the government tests are no further along than MAZE's and she has a funny feeling that Dr Cole's files may mysteriously become corrupted,' he winked in his sister's direction and she nodded her consent. He shared a conspiratorial glance with Alfie, and Lexi's shoulders sagged with relief.

'Mother Nature has decided that it takes two loving

parents to create a child now, not us. So we will leave it to Mother Nature to decide when, and if, everyone else finds out how we have evolved.'

'Do you think we'll all end up with gills in a hundred years and be able to breathe under water?' joked Lexi.

'You never know!' laughed David.

'I think our conclusion was right though. If you aren't going to give your child the love and support it needs, then the child won't be created. Parents might not always love each other, but unless they are going to love their child, then it seems that the child will never be born. I, for one, am glad about it and am so grateful that I found someone who I love, who loves me back and that we were able to create new life.' He looked at his little family and felt his heart swell with pride.

'We are seeing so many happier children, with parents who love and cherish them, through good times and bad, that it's not our decision to interfere, nor would we want to.'

'What about all of those people who want children but can't have them now?' asked Lexi.

'Maybe the gene will change over time and the cycle of life will begin again like it used to, but perhaps it won't. It's not for us to decide. It's part of who we are. Humankind has grown taller over the last 150 years and our life expectancy has skyrocketed from forty-five years to around one hundred. None of us know how the human race is evolving. We just have to embrace it as best we can.'

Tilly grasped his hand, letting him know that he had made the right decision to keep it to themselves, and let out the breath she had been holding. Alfie and Lexi nodded their approval. 'The future of mankind is down to the love of parents,' she whispered contentedly to her son. 'Do you think there will be someone else out there like Dr Cole who will want to cash in on the way we are evolving and to try and synthesize how we reproduce in the future?

'Probably,' said David. 'There will always be someone trying to control how people live and die, but like everything, we are changing and this is a change for the better. They have tried to interfere and create their own magic formulas for the people of the future, but none of them have worked. They won't find out anything from testing anyone, other than a new gene that could confound them for centuries. It's not been manufactured and it's not something we can avoid. It's a way of protecting the children of the future and making sure they are taken care of. Not only are the new children loved, but most people on this planet will be able to have a baby if they are going to love the child, which means lots of people will be happier. Those who are doing it for the wrong reasons will find themselves out in the cold. It's nature's way of protecting us all.'

David scooped his little family into his arms and couldn't wait for them to meet Poppy. He wouldn't have worried about her child being unwanted by her parents, as even without the gene, he had already seen how much she and Lucas cherished the addition to their new family. They would have quite a mess to sort out with Jemima and Mr Venner, but he thought they had the strength to get through it together.

He hoped he and Poppy could become a family again one day and perhaps they could all become involved in making sure nature's plans for them continued to unfold in the most natural way possible. If Abbigale had anything to do with it, she'd have them all working for her secret government agency before they'd set foot outside, he grinned, seeing Alfie looking restless and Lexi's shoulders slumping with exhaustion. It had been a long day for all of them and it was time to go home.

Tilly sighed and snuggled closer into his arms. 'All we need is each other,' she whispered, her eyes fluttering closed.

David looked round the room once more and his heart filled with such respect for everyone in the room. 'It's more than that,' he said. 'All you need is love...'

ACKNOWLEDGMENTS

A big thank you to my friends and family. I appreciate you for listening to my story ideas, never telling me to stop writing and for being an amazing group of people.

Thank you to my editor, Alice, who always has a kind word and offers me endless support on my writing journey. Publishing a book is a team effort and working with you is such a pleasure, Alice.

To my readers. Without you I wouldn't be able to keep writing. I appreciate you for picking up my books, for telling your friends and for the amazing reviews you write and share.

ABOUT THE AUTHOR

Award-winning inventor and author, Lizzie Chantree, started her own business at the age of 18 and became one of Fair Play London and The Patent Office's British Female Inventors of the Year in 2000. She discovered her love of writing fiction when her children were little and now runs networking hours on social media, where creative businesses, writers, photographers and designers can offer advice and support to each other. She lives with her family on the coast in Essex. Visit her website at www. lizziechantree.com or follow her on Twitter @Lizzie_Chantree

https://twitter.com/Lizzie_Chantree

I really hope you enjoyed reading Love's Child. It was an interesting and fun-filled book to write. If you liked reading my novel, please consider leaving a review. Many readers look to the reviews first when deciding which book to choose, and seeing your review might help them discover this one. I appreciate your help and support. Make an author smile today. Leave a review! Thank you so much. From Lizzie :)

PRAISE FOR LIZZIE CHANTREE

Nobody writes like Lizzie Chantree. You just know when you read a Lizzie Chantree book that you are going to enjoy it.

— BESTSELLING AUTHOR, ISABELLA MAY

If you haven't had the pleasure of reading one of Lizzie's books yet - treat yourself! She gives Jilly Cooper a run for your money in the racy stakes, coupled with the knowing charm of Jane Austen, in hilarious settings with characters that show contemporary chick-lit romances can hold their own when it comes to ballsy, brash behaviour!

— AUTHOR, JAN HAWKE

IF YOU LOVE ME, I'M YOURS.

WERE BONDS OF FRIENDSHIP, LOVE AND
LOYALTY, STRONG ENOUGH TO WITHSTAND
FAME, SUCCESS AND SCANDAL?

CHAPTER 1

Maud closed her eyes and prepared to jump off the emotional cliff she was teetering on the edge of. She shuffled forward until she felt sick with nerves, took a deep calming breath and waited.

'Oh, Maud...' her mother sighed. 'Not again.'

Maud cringed at the familiarity of those words, and in her mind, she stepped off into the void and plunged into the icy darkness without a whimper. In reality, she was still in her lounge, but being around her mother made her feel like an abject failure and the words she uttered sliced through Maud and filled her with doom. Her mum pushed her to the edge of reason on a regular basis. She wished that for once her mother could try harder to be nice. Surely it couldn't be that difficult to be grateful for the anniversary gift she had been given and to offer a smile, even a fake one, for the sake of her child? It was the same every year and Maud was finally ready to surrender and stop trying so hard to make them understand her and compliment one of her paintings. It was never going to happen, she realised with a heavy heart.

Maud didn't mind being boring, not really. She had a sensible job, sensible clothes, a sensible love life... if you counted two overbearing exes and a one night stand who had thanked her, rolled over and was snoring before she even realised he had started! She was ok with not fulfilling her dreams or being outrageous and carefree, she just wanted her parents to pay her a compliment, just once, after years of disapproval and disappointment.

Maud knew that as far as her mum was concerned, she was the most amazing parent who encouraged her daughter to have a responsible career until she settled down and found a 'suitable' husband. Granted, Maud was a very good, well-liked and adept teacher's assistant in the local primary school, but every time she pushed against the boundaries set by her parents for their perfect daughter... *'Oh, Maud!'*

It was ridiculous, she was twenty-four, thought Maud. She wished she had a big glass of wine to slug back, but her mother would disapprove of that too, suggest in horror that she was a 'wino,' and hand her the number for AA, which she would have readily available in the little brown Filofax she carried everywhere in her patent handbag. The woman was a menace.

'You don't like the painting, then?' she asked. Her mother tilted her head to one side without a word, her lip between her teeth as she concentrated and her brow furrowing as she looked at the artwork in confusion. It wasn't the reaction Maud had hoped for. She had spent hours delicately drawing the lines of the little landscape painting of her parents' house and she felt salty tears scratch her eyes. She refused to let them spill out in front of her mother, though, and bit her own lip until she tasted blood. The painting wasn't Maud's preferred style, spidery black lines depicting beautiful animals, filled in with splashes of vibrant colourwork to bring them to life. She had hoped that by toning down her eclectic style and drawing such a personal space as her parents' home, her mother would finally see the little girl who desperately wanted to paint.

Her father coughed into his hand and looked at his daughter. 'Well...' Maud's heart almost stopped beating in her chest as she waited to hear his response to her work. She turned towards him with unshed tears in eyes shining with hope. He had seen this look so many times and she knew that he hated to disappoint her, but her mum would make his life a living hell if he encouraged her. Her mum saw anything creative as frivolous and a waste of time, and generally her dad agreed with her. He said quietly to her sometimes that he appreciated that Maud enjoyed painting, but her art wasn't exactly going to set the world ablaze with awe at her talents, now was it? The words had cut into her heart and she'd cringed in pain. She knew he felt that it certainly wasn't appropriate for a serious young lady who wanted to teach children and catch a husband. The thought of her attracting a layabout artist and spending her days smoking spliffs must horrify him, as he often left articles about wild artists who were living outrageous lives around the house when she visited. He must have gone out to buy the magazines especially, as her mother would never leave anything out on the table otherwise, she was such a neat freak. Maud sometimes wondered how many hours he must spend sifting through the shelves at the newsagents, as how many articles about wild and out of control artists could there be? Maybe he stored them in the garage in a cardboard box? She had never actually picked one up, as that would fuel their obsession. Perhaps he just recycled the same article? She'd have to pay more attention next time.

He moved to the edge of his seat to scrutinise the little

work of art and scratched his head in obvious confusion. She hoped he could see it was quite pretty and that Maud had obviously spent much of her free time on it. She could imagine the thoughts in his head, like where would they put such a colourful picture on their mostly beige walls? He looked across at her and must have noticed the unshed tears in her eyes. 'I wish with all my heart that I could see what you do, but art is a complete mystery to me,' he sighed. 'I'm not one for artsy stuff. We have racks of your paintings in the spare room from when you were younger. I've put up shelves in there,' he paused and she could almost hear him add *to hide them away*, 'but we do appreciate the effort you put in and are grateful for this year's anniversary present, darling.'

Maud was sure he couldn't help but notice that she was almost hopping from foot to foot in agitation and her eyes were bright with questions. He looked pained, as if his guts had just turned over. She knew her mum would hide this little painting in the spare room as soon as possible after she had stepped through the front door at home, but hopefully he could see how much it meant to Maud. He gritted his teeth and her heart melted as his shoulders straightened and he stood a bit taller. She could see that he'd decided that for once he was going to stand his ground. 'It's pretty, love.' Maud let out the breath she'd been holding and rushed over to squeeze the life out of her dad in her excitement, until he was laughing and gasping for air.

'But...' interrupted Rosemary, getting up. Maud wondered if she had told her dad not to react when Maud gave them another painting and finally to talk her out of this most unsuitable habit. 'For goodness sake, Maud! You're a teacher with lots of other ways to fill your days. Why are you mucking about with paints when you should be trying to find a husband?' Maud's smile dropped from her face and her dad looked upset. She could feel the gloom returning.

'It's pretty,' he repeated firmly, making Rosemary sit back down in confusion at his forceful tone. 'We can put it by the window in the kitchen so that we can look at it every day.'

Rosemary's face went white with shock and she looked like she might faint at the thought of that monstrosity in her pristine cream kitchen, but one glance at her husband silenced her protest. She lifted her face and saw Maud's slightly unkempt hair and wild eyes and her face softened slightly.

'I don't know why it means so much to you for us to have some of your pictures, but maybe we can find a corner for this one if it's that important. I'm not a monster. I don't know where you get this painting thing from, Maud,' she added, getting up and running her hands down Maud's soft blond hair to straighten out the kinks.

Maud dressed impeccably in neutral tones and her hair didn't usually have a strand out of place, as she tamed the unruly curls at the ends with hot hair straighteners every day. Even her bungalow, with its stark white walls and modern but functional furniture, was always immaculately clean, even if it was a strange choice of home for such a young woman. Maud's mum didn't really have anything to complain about, as Maud did everything in her power to please her parents, other than this one small thing. For some reason her mum had a deep rooted fear that Maud needed to be kept under control in case she started running around naked or dying her hair pink, orange and blue again, like she had as a child.

Rosemary often recalled the memory to Maud. She blamed her own older sister, Maud's aunt – whom she too often referred to as 'the annoying one' – for starting this mess by buying her then five-year-old niece a set of colourful finger paints. For the next few years it had been chaos. Rosemary said her stomach often turned over at the recollection. The beautifully clean walls of their three-bedroom terraced home were spattered with every colour of the rainbow, as Maud decided that they should be 'smiley colours.' Her clothes, which her mum spent hours laundering and ironing, began to be covered with pen and ink blobs and smears, which were the faces of their pedigree, non-shedding cat and his rather less salubrious neighbourhood friends. Every surface Maud could find followed suit.

Her mum had initially thought that it was a phase that Maud would grow out of, and yelled at her sister for being so bloody inconsiderate. She got haughty distain in return, and it explained why they still couldn't stand being in the same room together. As Maud grew up, she learnt not to paint on the surfaces of her home lest she invoke the wrath of her parents, but she began doing odd jobs for extra pocket money and bought paper, pens and an art folder to hide under her bed. Within weeks it had been full to bursting and her mum had wrung her hands in despair at the clutter and nearly kicked the poor cat as she constantly tripped over tubes of paint, which had escaped from the desk drawer. Admittedly, Maud's room was mostly tidy, but her homework desk overflowed with art supplies and the smell of fresh paint now made her mum feel faint.

Over the years, Maud had realised that her art was a frivolity and she had gradually dwindled to painting only occasionally, until she had stopped altogether. Now she had her own private space, the 'phase' had begun again, and her mum was distraught. At least the mess was at Maud's own house and she didn't have much time to paint now she had a full-time job.

'You do seem to be happy here,' Rosemary sighed, looking around at Maud's home and mentioning that the kitchen cupboards needed rubbing down and repainting. She watched Maud as she leaned forward and hugged her dad again, dodging away from her mum's hands, as Rosemary tried to brush a speck of dust from her soft blue jumper and then tugged at the hem of her skirt to straighten it.

'Thanks, dad,' Maud beamed at him, generously turning and enveloping her mother in the hug too, making her blush furiously and shoosh her away.

CHAPTER 2

Dot straightened one of the five pigtails on top of her head and made sure they were sticking out at the right angle. She moved the chunky jewellery she was wearing to the correct spot on one side of her neck and patted down her checked skirt and sparkly blue tights.

She glanced around to assure herself that everything was in place and the paintings were lit properly. The drinks were all set out along the temporary bar, which was actually her receptionist's desk; glasses sparkled and surfaces shone with the elbow grease that had gone into making this evening perfect. Tonight was a big deal for her and the largest art show she had personally organised. Working as creative director for her parents and big brother was lively and interesting, but her soul cried out to be part of the inner circle of artists, rather than on the outside echelons as their manager. She knew she was brilliant at her job, but her family was a dynasty of talented artists and she was the oddity, the black sheep with colourful hair.

Dot adored painting, but unfortunately she was completely atrocious at it. It was hopeless. She didn't just stink at painting; she was abysmal; a word she'd heard whispered about her work by a visiting uncle en route to his latest exhibition. The look of pity on her parents' faces when they scrutinised her painterly offerings, and the confusion in her brother's eyes when he tried to find a meaning in the splotches and swirls, were enough to make her hang her head in shame. As a consolation, and to make her feel involved when she was old enough, they had kindly offered her the chance to manage their work, as she had the advantage of understanding them all so well. She had taken on the role after much persuasion and a little emotional blackmail over their hurt feelings and she was determined to make everyone see she was one of them.

She dressed accordingly for someone who was part of the art community, with zany and outrageous clothes, and worked determinedly to ensure her family's art was seen all over the world and reached markets and customers they had never considered before. They had been suitably astounded as, satisfyingly, she was surprisingly good at her job. She handled their work with flair and was a real asset to them, but as a failed artist and family member, Dotty still felt that she had something to prove, however much they told her she was irreplaceable.

Anyone could sell art this good, surely? thought Dot.

Out of the corner of her eye she spotted a light above her brother's second piece of work flicker and die. All of his creativity was dark and stormy and the public went mad over his brooding good looks and grumpy demeanour. She loved him dearly... but what the hell was all that about?

She could see the appeal of his art; it was sublime, but her brother was not the best advertisement for relationships. Women flocked to his feet, but he could barely remember their names and left her fielding calls from the moment she arrived at the gallery each morning. The fact that he only gave them his work number should have alerted them to his intentions, but they all thought he was worth mooning by the phone for. Yuck. It was almost enough to put her off dating for life... almost.

CHAPTER 3

Maud reverently stroked the embossed surface of the invitation she was holding to a private gallery viewing later that evening. She'd visited many galleries over the years, but none so glamorous or exciting as this one. The Ridgemoors were world famous artists, and attaining a ticket to the preview show was like getting back stage passes to an Ed Sheeran concert and being allowed to snog his face off afterwards.

Maud's best friend Daisy had forced her to go alone tonight, which wasn't very kind of her. Maud had claimed one of the prizes in an art competition, which she hadn't even known she'd entered, as her friend was a common thief and had stolen one of her little paintings and entered it without Maud's knowledge.

When it had won, Daisy had plied Maud with alcohol at the local pub, which Maud should have instantly found suspicious as Daisy hardly ever bought a round of drinks, and then confessed to stealing her work. Maud was slightly mollified by the fact that it had won a prize and even she couldn't turn down the opportunity of getting so close to one of Nate Ridgemoor's paintings.

The prize for her winning entry was one precious ticket to the private view. She grudgingly accepted that Daisy thought she was helping her to get out and meet new people. Then her best friend had called her that evening and put on what Maud could only describe as the worst acting she had ever heard, coughing and spluttering that she couldn't drive her to the viewing, which was Maud's stipulation for accepting the invitation, even though Daisy had been perfectly fine earlier in the day at work. Daisy thought Maud's knickers were made of concrete as they were so tough to get into, and she was desperate for Maud to meet a man. She used every excuse to dump her alone somewhere, even if it meant her getting the train on her own at night.

Daisy was one of the few people that Maud had confided in about her own love of painting, although even she hadn't seen Maud's latest work. The art she had submitted on Maud's behalf was pretty enough, but it wasn't her usual style at all. Nonetheless, the turbulent seascape had won a prize and the expensive invitation in her hand had arrived with a letter saying her work had shown promise and that she had been one of five entries selected to win tickets to the private view.

Maud remembered how Daisy had danced around the simple room when they had arrived back at her bungalow and she'd realised that Maud wasn't about to dive over the table to strangle her for being so deceitful. She'd tried in vain to entice Maud to bring some of the vibrant cushions she had strewn across her hand-sewn bedspread into the lounge, to brighten the place up, but Maud had remained resolute that it was unnecessary and would give her mother a heart attack when she visited.

Luckily, Rosemary had never ventured into Maud's bedroom or seen the serene forest mural on the wall. Daisy said she thought this was strange, but Maud just shrugged, as if the fact didn't hurt, and mumbled that they didn't have that kind of girly relationship. Daisy often wondered aloud if Maud actually wanted her mum to poke her nose around the house and take an interest in the way her daughter expressed her true personality, with the vibrant colours and fabrics she had hidden away. Daisy thought she wanted to shock Rosemary, but anyway, the moment had never materialised, as her mum was too focussed on how neat the kitchen was or if Maud's clothes were ironed to perfection while she was wearing them.

Maud kept her bedroom door firmly shut and her mum never expressed an interest in staying too long, before busily pronouncing she had somewhere else to be. Rosemary enjoyed Maud visiting her own house, but only at the most convenient times, preferably when there was someone else there for her to brag to about Maud's teaching career, which made Maud cringe in embarrassment as she'd had the same job for ages now and hadn't bothered to apply for anything else. Maud wished she had a brother or sister to confide in, but that was her fault too. She had been so messy and inconsiderate as a child that her mother had told her that she couldn't cope with more children like her.

Maud slid open the door to her wardrobe and ran her hand along her collection of rich, textural fabrics hidden inside. Sighing heavily, she slid the door further along and grimaced at the rows of bland tops, skirts and dresses. Her fingers itched to grab something frivolous, but the vision of her mother's angry face and bugged-out eyes always stopped her.

Maud hated her magpie tendencies to buy beautiful,

sparkly clothes, as she'd never wear any of them. She just couldn't walk past a shop window and not bring them home; she had to have them, even if it was just to look at. Reaching out and selecting a simple black dress, she stuck her tongue out at her reflection in the mirror in the en-suite bathroom and hung the offending dress up on the back of the door, before turning on the shower to warm the water up a little.

Towelling her hair dry after an invigorating shower, she plugged in her hair straighteners and watched the tiny light on the side turn green. She had to get up half an hour early every morning to tame her hair and tonight she needed to get a move on if she was going to arrive on time. She was the only person she knew with straight, curly hair. Her hair was completely poker straight until it reached just below her ears, then it sprung into unruly curls. What the hell was all that about? She was sure her hair was rebelling and wished she had the courage to do the same.

She couldn't have a perm as her hair wanted to be straight and it didn't take hold. The bottom section could be straightened, but as her hair was thick and golden-blonde, this took forever to get right. She grabbed the irons, narrowly missing scorching her hand, and began the laborious process of taming the curls into submission.

Available from Amazon.